"Sharp dialogue, fully fleshed, interesting characters, and a believable plot add up to more than typical teen chicklit." —*Quill & Quire*

"*Leading Lines* is a great follow-up to the previous two Pippa Greene novels and takes her story deeper into her personal life and into her genuine love for her family, her friends, and her photography . . . These novels remain relatable and sweet and are a great read for anyone looking for dynamic and honest relationships in their YA fiction." —*Read My Breath Away*

"Effortless, light and rewarding, this is a series that readers could grasp starting with this third book, but it's worthwhile to get all three and get to know the bubbly, endearing, lovable Pippa from the beginning." —*Globe and Mail*

"This third of the planned four-book Pippa Greene series is a manual in how romantic relationships can derail on the realities of everyday life. . . . The style is lively and teens will sympathize with the misunderstandings and doubts that can fracture a relationship." —*VOYA Magazine*

"Teens will readily relate with Pippa who is an engaging, complex 16-year-old . . . Readers might not always like Pippa or agree with her choices, but everything she says and does rings completely true. Readers will experience all the joys, heartbreak and discoveries of the teenage years as Pippa continues her journey to adulthood. With this series, Guertin has written another novel with a plot that is believable but not predictable, a rare treat in young adult fiction." —*CM: Canadian Review of Materials*

DEPTH OF FIELD

"Amusingly honest . . . Frothy yet engaging romance with a
snapshot of the photography world to add color." —*Kirkus Reviews*

"With an upbeat tone, clever dialogue and an artsy
point of view, *Depth of Field* is one relatable teenage girl's
contemporary coming-of-age journey." —*School Library Journal*

"Tight plotting, vivid characters and an underlying
thread of photography know-how make *Depth of Field* a smart and
stylish read." —*National Reading Campaign*

"Guertin truly inhabits the world of a talented 16-year-old who, in
spite of self-doubt, faces the world head on. And if the story is one
that has been told many times, many ways, Guertin's approach to it is
creative and new." —*CM: Canadian Review of Materials*

"It's nice to see a heroine who has both feet on the ground. She's
genuine: with one foot she steps out to the future; the other clawing
her back as she deals with the personal loss. Pippa is not the clichéd
heroine you'd expect in a YA novel." —*Sukasa Reads*

"Just as emotional of a read as the last book . . . sweet and touching."
—*Words of Mystery*

"Anyone who is looking for some quick and fun reads but still wants
to find a reason to get invested in a story and a character's journey
needs to look no further than Guertin's Pippa Greene series."
—*Read My Breath Away*

"If you enjoy realistic YA fiction with an authentic voice, I'd recommend
this series." —*Ramblings of a Daydreamer*

"Pippa is an appealing heroine and this will find readers." —*Voya*

THE RULE OF THIRDS

"The story flows nicely, has believable characters and will appeal
to readers looking for a realistic tale with a bit of romance."
—*School Library Journal*

"If you like stories about trying to find yourself while dealing with
the ultimate grief of losing a parent, like Eileen Cool's *Unraveling
Isobel*, then you won't be able to put this one down." —*Faze Magazine*

"Chantel Guertin has created a loveable character with Pippa Greene,
and a loveable book with *The Rule of Thirds*." —Alice Kuipers, author
of *40 Things I Want to Tell You*

"As an angsty teen I could have used a heroine as smart, funny and,
most importantly, as imperfect as Pippa to give voice to all of my own
complicated feelings about growing up. *The Rule of Thirds* captures
perfectly the balancing act between vulnerability and bravado of
teenage life." —Ceri Marsh, co-author of *The Fabulous Girl's Guide
to Decorum*

"Part romance, part tearjerker, part friendship story—this terrific read
will capture your heart." —Sarah Mlynowski, author of *Ten Things We
Did (and Probably Shouldn't Have)*

"Chantel Guertin creates a realistic, poignant story about loss, love,
friendship and finding light in darkness. *The Rule of Thirds* is a fresh,
endearing novel that will capture your heart, expose a smile, and
stay in your memory like a favorite family photo." —Laura Bowers,
author of *Beauty Shop* and *Just Flirt*

"With clever twists that kept me reading, *The Rule of Thirds* is
a beautifully written novel that explores real-life issues
through the eyes of a teenager. Once I started, I couldn't put it down."
—Heather A. Clark, author of *Chai Tea Sunday*

"Chantel Guertin [balances] fears, grief, romance, friendship, angst,
ambitions and common sense, in different proportions to produce a
picture that works." —*CanLit for Little Canadians*

"A major plot twist doesn't involve friend drama and has little to do with boys, which is hard to find in YA. Also rare is how realistically Pippa is drawn . . . she's presented as capable, thoughtful, and intellectual without being clichéd." —*Quill & Quire*

"Guertin's voice is impeccable, believably channeling a 16-year-old girl who must learn the uncomfortable reality that life is not a fairytale, and not all stories end happily ever after. The resulting novel is surprisingly upbeat as Pippa copes with normal life marching on—often with hilarious results." —National Reading Campaign

"*The Rule of Thirds* ventures beyond the mundane comforts of the average teenage problem novel, and instead, explores deeper issues using a creative plot and a flowing narrative, helping to solidify this novel as a well-rounded and engaging option for readers. Recommended." —*CM: Canadian Review of Materials*

"You'll fall in love with this genuine young heroine as she experiences the ups and downs of being a teen while dealing with the loss of her dad." —*Best Health*

GOLDEN HOUR

A PIPPA GREENE NOVEL

Chantel Guertin

ECW Press

Published by ECW Press
665 Gerrard Street East
Toronto, ON M4M 1Y2
416-694-3348 / info@ecwpress.com

Library and Archives Canada
Cataloguing in Publication

Guertin, Chantel, 1976–, author
Golden hour : a Pippa Greene novel /
Chantel Guertin.

Issued in print and electronic formats.
ISBN 978-1-77041-235-4 (softcover)
ISBN 978-1-77305-144-4 (PDF)
978-1-77305-143-7 (ePUB)

I. Title.

PS8637.I474G65 2018   C813'.6
C2017-906215-8   C2017-906216-6

Editor for the press: Crissy Calhoun
Cover images: Shutterstock;
crazystocker
Author photo: Mango Studios

The publication of *Golden Hour* has been generously supported by the Canada Council for the Arts which last year invested $153 million to bring the arts to Canadians throughout the country, and by the Government of Canada through the Canada Book Fund. *Nous remercions le Conseil des arts du Canada de son soutien. L'an dernier, le Conseil a investi 153 millions de dollars pour mettre de l'art dans la vie des Canadiennes et des Canadiens de tout le pays. Ce livre est financé en partie par le gouvernement du Canada.* We also acknowledge the Ontario Arts Council (OAC), an agency of the Government of Ontario, and the contribution of the Government of Ontario through the Ontario Book Publishing Tax Credit and the Ontario Media Development Corporation.

PRINTED AND BOUND IN CANADA BY MARQUIS   5   4   3   2   1

RECYCLED
Paper made from
recycled material
FSC   FSC® C103567
www.fsc.org

For my sister, Danielle

"Did you hear about Emma?" I say as Dace pulls out of the school parking lot and onto Elm Street. Despite its name, Elm Street is actually lined with cherry blossom trees, and they're in full bloom, dotting the afternoon sky with pinks and whites.

Dace is bopping her head to the music that's blaring from the new speaker system her stepdad installed in her white Fiat 500, the car her mom and stepdad bought her after The Incident. She shakes her head, her blonde ponytail swishing, and turns down the volume. She slows to a stop at the red light and turns to look at me. "What about her?"

"Brown. She got in."

"Eek. But please don't be blue about Brown," she says, giving me a bright smile. I know she's just trying to make me laugh, but it's not working. She knows that every time one of our classmates gets an acceptance, I retreat a little further into my den of doom. I still haven't heard a peep out of Tisch.

"I'm more like green. With envy. Also, the light." I point to the stoplight.

Dace hits the gas, then taps the screen on the dashboard and the sound of loons and trickling water fills the car. "You need a Zen moment."

I make a face. Dace found Buddha in January, and now she's all boho hippie. Which means she wears a lot of embroidered tunics and floral kaftans and says things like "Find your inner calm" and "Be mindful."

Dace taps her gold nails on the steering wheel. She still paints her nails and wears hot pink lipstick though. She's a girl in transition, figuring out her new post-model identity. "Isn't this making you feel better?"

"It's making me have to pee."

"So what if Emma got into Brown? You don't want to go to Brown. You didn't even apply to Brown. You don't even know where Brown is." She smacks her hot pink lips together as though to punctuate her point.

"Providence, Rhode Island, actually."

"Noted. Point is, I bet you're going to hear from Tisch any day now."

"Uh huh." I pull my phone out of my black back-pack and click on the email icon for the 427th time today. My phone pings every time I get a new email, but obviously I can't rely on technology, so I just check it manually every three to five minutes. Or so. When we're not in class, that is, due to the super-frustrating rule that we can't use our phones in class.

My inbox refreshes. Nothing. I shove my phone back into my bag.

"If you happen to see my mom, don't mention Brown. I fake applied to Brown."

"Oh. My. Gotthard. You and the fake applying. I don't know how you keep it all straight."

"Gotthard?"

"Gotthard Base Tunnel. Longest train tunnel in the world. It's in the Swiss Alps."

Ever since Dace decided she was going to take a gap year to travel after graduation, she's been full of travel facts. We're going to backpack together for a month this summer, before I go to Tisch. *If* I get into Tisch. Usually I find her fun facts amusing, except when I'm in a bad mood about college. Which seems like most of the time, lately. Sometimes I wish I could be like Dace and take a slacker year to live life, but it's just not me. To put off real life for a whole year. But of course I've never told her I think that. Or that I secretly call it a slacker year.

"What *are* you going to do when your mom starts asking why you haven't received your acceptances from the colleges you fake applied to?" Dace makes a right onto Calcutta and slows down as a couple of kids cross the street up ahead.

"As soon as I get my offer from Tisch, my mom'll forget all about the other schools. Hopefully." I hold my crossed fingers in the air.

"And then you can end your Black Period and start having fun again? Because between your all-work attitude and your all-black clothes, you've been kind of a buzzkill these past few months. Still my best friend, and totally understandable, but—a buzzkill. Remember, I'm supposed to be all Good Vibes Only–ing."

"May I point out that my Black Period is less a state of mind than a state of style? So you shouldn't let my outfits get to you. Every legit photographer, ever, wears black. It's the unofficial uniform. Like saying, 'Don't worry, this pic I'm taking? It's not for likes.'"

Dace exhales dramatically. "You and your Insta judginess." She's teasing, but it's definitely a bit of a touchy subject. Photography was always *my* thing. But now it feels like everyone thinks they're a photographer, just because they have an iPhone and an Instagram account. Which wouldn't be so bad except that no one cares about anything that actually goes into taking a good photo: lighting, composition, depth of field, rule of thirds. Nothing. Just faux-arty shoe snaps with a filter slapped on and they get a bazillion likes. And if they don't? Delete. It's *so* irritating. My Instagram grid is the exact opposite.

"Also, I *had* to get serious this year. That's how you get good grades, good enough SAT scores and a half-decent portfolio to send to Tisch. This is the dream, Dace. The *dream*."

In retrospect, it probably wasn't the *best* idea to only apply to Tisch but at the time, I thought I was making a strategic move. And it wasn't about the application fees. Or the work it takes to apply. It was the fact that I don't want to go to any other schools, so why should I make up some reason on my essay that I want to go, and then possibly get accepted and then cause someone else total misery because they didn't get into the only school they ever wanted to go to, because I did. Not applying was actually an act of public service, thank you very much. Also I had this thought like, What if colleges can tell which other schools you applied to, and so when they saw that I only applied to Tisch they'd know how serious I was, and then maybe that would work in my favor. Only apparently that's not how it works. I sort of mentioned something about it to Mr. Aquila, our guidance counselor, who set me straight. And then I just pretended I totally knew that anyway.

Dace pulls into my driveway, puts the car in park and swivels in her seat to face me. "All right, I take your point. All I'm saying is I can't wait until you get that acceptance so we can spend the rest of our senior year goofing off and making bad decisions."

I unbuckle my seatbelt and give her a sidelong look. "Thanks for the ride."

"See you later, Darth."

Once I'm through the front door, I kick off my black leather high-tops. The house is quiet, and I remember that Mom is working the four-to-midnight shift tonight. When my stomach unclenches, I realize how tense I've been since leaving school. I walk into the kitchen to grab a glass of orange juice. There's a vase filled with lilacs on the kitchen table. I've been doing this thing with my Instagram feed, where I choose a color for the week and each day I post a shot of something that color. (Except Sundays when I don't post because seven shots screws up my feed, whereas six shots looks perfect.) I don't get many likes, despite all my deliberation, but I just haven't found my audience yet. I'm building my brand, and it'll all pay off in a few years when I'm surrounded by real photographers in New York. Anyway, this week I'm shooting purples. I already have my shot for today, ready to edit before posting, but the lavender flowers, shot against the white wall behind the kitchen table with the natural light streaming in through the back patio doors, would make a really clean, gorgeous shot to post later in the week. I pull a few stems out of the vase. As I do, a small white card drops to the table, face up. I tilt my head to read the message.

Holly,

You're the best thing that's happened to me.

Happy 15th monthiversary.

All my love, Hank

Ick.

Monthiversary? Double ick.

Also, when the flowers for your mom are from your English Lit teacher? Triple ick.

I grab my camera from my backpack and try to block out the fact that my mom and Hank's relationship is apparently still super hot. Then I arrange the flowers into a cluster and hold the stems with my left hand, my camera with my right. I'm usually all about the rule of thirds in photos, but sometimes, rules are meant to be broken, and I frame the shot so that the flowers are perfectly centered, my arm a leading line from the bottom left-hand corner to the center of the photo. I snap off a dozen shots, making small tweaks with the angles and the flowers, and then scroll back through the photos to see the results. Satisfied, I replace the flowers in the vase, nestle the card into the petals and take a sip of orange juice. As usual, taking a photo has calmed me. I put my camera back in my bag and head upstairs just as my phone dings. Hands shaking, I pull out my phone and touch the mail icon.

From: admissions@tisch.org
Subject: Status on your application

You have a change in the status of one or more of your applications. Please log in to your account using the link below.

I put a hand out. The wall accepts my weight, which is lucky because otherwise I'd be a heap on the carpet. Should I call Dace? I should call Dace. The silence of the house is overwhelming. She'd probably find it Zen. Meanwhile how awful would it be if the email says no? No, they don't want me, no, I'm not getting in, and all around me was the Zen silence cut only by my many, many sobs?

It just takes a moment to log in.

Status on application to Tisch School of the Arts: Waitlisted

Wait—*what?*

And below, the letter. Key words jump out immediately, as if typed in bolder font than the rest.

Regret

Unfortunately

Unable

Best of luck

My back hits the wall, my butt hits the floor. The room gets all wavy as my eyes get wet. I close my eyes. I have to tell Mom. I need to tell Mom. Even if it means telling her everything—that I have no backup plan. My phone's still in my hand; she's the first on my Favorites. It rings and rings and then goes to her voicemail. I hang up and then open the text bubble.

My hands shake too much to type out the word *waitlisted*. Do I just tell her I didn't get in? Because isn't that essentially what waitlisted means? Who's going to *turn down* a spot in the best photography program in the country so that I can get in? I decide to just tell her that I know. That I got the email. I can explain the rest when I see her.

Me: I got it.

I hit send and toss my phone on the floor beside me then lean forward, closing my eyes and pressing my face into my knees to block out any possible light.

My phone rings and I lift my head and grab my phone. Mom. I click Accept but before I can say anything she is squealing in my ear. Black spots appear before my eyes. I have broken her.

"Mom?" I say tentatively.

"Oh Pippa, I'm soooooo proud of you! I just knew you could do it. All your hard work and your focus and your dedication. At times I thought, Oh gosh, do I need to help her to expand her interests a little because, you know, you can be *so* into photography, but you knew. You knew that all that focus and shutting out everything else would be exactly what you needed to get in. And Tisch! Tisch, Pippa! Your father would be so proud of you. I know it shouldn't matter, and of course I would've been proud of you if you had gotten into one of your other schools—but oh it's just like you really are following in his footsteps, and it's just . . ." She sighs. "It makes me feel like a bit of your father is with us right now. Like you're carrying a piece of him with you." She rambles on while I listen, speechless. How am I going to interrupt her, correct her to tell her that she has it wrong, that I didn't get in. Finally she says she has a dog with three legs to see but we will celebrate later. She hangs up and I pull the phone away from my ear. My text is still there on the screen. I stare at it in disbelief.

I got in.

The message from me says *I got in*, not *I got it*.

I'm leaning against my locker, soggy and uncomfortable because I walked to school in the rain, when
Dace saunters up in a long, flowy dress and Birks
with slouchy rainbow socks, which only she can pull
off, and a massive purple backpack that practically
runs the entire length of her body, which is saying
something because she's five foot eleven. A pair of
brand new hot pink hiking boots dangle on the side,
and there's a purple ombre S'well bottle in the side
pocket. She's swinging her collapsed umbrella.

"Where were you this morning? I stopped by
your house to give you a ride but your mom said
you left before she even woke up."

"What's with the backpack?"

"I see you're fully implementing the avoidance
technique. So you walked to school in a torrential
downpour instead? You seriously need to get your

license. I don't understand how times like this don't motivate you to just book the test. Then we could just make like Thelma and Louise this summer. Drive across America. Open road. Wind in our hair. Minus the murder and running from the cops part."

On the long list of things I've cut out of my life this year—part-time job, guys, *fun*—is taking my driving test. After I had to retake my SATs to get my score up to 1250 from 900, the last thing I wanted to add to my list of failures was my driver's test. Plus, there was this little voice in the back of my mind that kept reminding me that I'd be spending the next four years in New York, and what good would a driver's license do in a city where no one drives?

"At least I got exercise," I grumble.

"When are you going to tell your mom?" After getting off the phone with Mom last night, I called Dace to tell her about the whole Tisch email and the Mom mistype.

"I dunno, 2043? Never? So what's with the pack?"

"That was a smooth pivot, but I'll take it. Isn't it *so me*?" Dace turns from side to side, as though modeling her new backpack. "Cost me 200 dollars but I think it is worth *every* dollar. I picked it up at REI last night. I read that if you're planning to back-pack, you should actually practice walking around with your backpack on. You know, so you don't pull a muscle or something. Remember that scene in *Wild* where she was just *so* tired from carrying her pack and her toe was bleeding and then her hiking boot fell over the cliff? PSA for being prepared." She gives the pack a little bump up and tightens the straps. "You should get one too. Then we can be backpack besties."

"Yeah," I say, but I get this pain like a small rodent is eating through my stomach from the inside out. The plan has always been to backpack for a month this summer, then Dace would continue backpacking while I came back, got ready for college and moved to New York. But that was when I was going to Tisch and hoped to get a scholarship. Even if I somehow get into Tisch, a scholarship's going to be totally out of the question, so that travel money I'd saved up from birthdays and Christmases? I'm going to need that to pay for tuition and rent and food and a phone plan, not flitting around Europe for a month. Not that the money I've saved up is going to cover even a teensy tiny portion of that. Ugh.

"So, you're going to carry your entire locker around all day?" I fiddle with my lock. Now is not the time to bring any of this up with Dace.

"God, no. Why would I do that? For one thing, textbooks are way too heavy. And it's not like I'm going to be backpacking with books. I filled it with all my favorite clothes. And beauty products. Ooh, that reminds me. I got you something." She reaches into a side pocket and pulls out a small pink lipgloss. "Teensy tiny cosmetics. Isn't it adorable? From now on, everything I buy is going to be teensy tiny. Even my underwear. Thongs all the time. To make more space for shoes."

"Thanks," I say, taking the lipgloss tube and turning it over. "At least I can look pretty when I'm working at the gas station next year."

Dace makes a face. "You are *not* going to be working at a gas station. In fact, I already have a plan for you. Are you ready to hear it?"

"Does it involve me going to Tisch?" I shove my backpack in my locker and grab my purple binder.

"No. Even better. You're going to forget all about college, take a gap year and backpack *with me*." Dace holds her hands up in the air, like she's just won a race. "Best. Idea. Ever. Amiright?"

I give her a weak smile and shake my head. "*Domo arigato*, but I can't do it. I can't afford it, and I can't give up on Tisch. Not yet." I point to her S'well bottle. "Can I borrow that for a second?"

Dace shrugs and hands me the bottle. "What for?"

"The 'gram." I pull everything off the top shelf of my locker and place the purple binder and Dace's water bottle on the shelf. I unzip my pencil case and pull out a couple of purple pencil crayons I use in Geography class, and line them up on the shelf, points sticking out. Then I hold my camera up high to get a straight-on shot. I snap a pic, check the result and make a few adjustments, forcing the aperture since the fluorescent hallway light isn't the best.

I can feel Dace's impatience growing, but she knows not to interrupt me when I'm in photo mode. I cap my camera and she dives back in. "OK so then what's your plan that's better than my plan?"

"Well, it's multi-step. Step one is to make a plan."

"Good plan."

"Help?"

"Of course." The bell rings. "Gotta go if I'm going

to make it to homeroom with this on my back. See you at lunch."

• • •

"There seems to be some sort of trend here, of pretending to go to Tisch," Dace says. We're in the far corner of the caf, away from everyone so we can talk in private; our lunches sit untouched in front of us. I've just read her the list of ideas I came up with in second period—which ranges from continuing to pretend to Mom that I got into Tisch while moving to New York and getting a job instead, to pretending to be a student at Tisch and sneaking into the photography classes. "I wonder if we need to broaden the scope of ideas here . . . You know, like, maybe we could figure out other photography programs that still have space?"

I shake my head and pop a fry into my mouth. "I don't want to go anywhere else. You know this. Tisch has been The Plan since *forever*."

Dace takes a sip of water and then opens her container of vanilla yogurt, and I steer my attention to my own lunch so Dace won't feel scrutinized. Still, my BFF radar is on high alert since she still has good and bad days when it comes to food.

"Listen, I get having the 'since forever' plan. You don't have to explain that to me. I, of anyone— *anyone*—get that. But if this past year has taught me anything, it's that sometimes you have to face reality. And when your dream and your reality aren't meeting up"—she puts down her spoon, then pretends to high five herself, her right and left hand totally missing each other—"maybe it's time to figure out a plan B."

Last summer, Dace met with her agent to talk about next steps—she was planning to move to New York to model after graduation, and she wanted to get on the radar of designers early so she could be booked during New York Fashion Week in September.

But her agent told her she wasn't going to put her forward for shows. That while she's tall and thin and gorgeous, she's not quite tall enough, quite thin enough or quite the right look for high fashion or glossy editorial spreads, and that the best she could expect to do with her look was the online shopping sites she was already doing. Dace didn't take the news well. I mean, who would? Since the only part of her agent's comments she could control was her weight, she threw herself into a really scary starvation period that got so bad that one morning she passed out while driving to school. She just missed a telephone pole, *thank god*, but she did crash her mom's car into a hedge. Luckily, she emerged from the accident unscathed, while making it totally clear to all of us that she was really *not* OK. Her mom checked her into Crestwood, this rehab center in Buffalo.

Feeling like I was the only one she could turn to, I took the bus to visit her every single Sunday, promising myself I would study for my SATs on the ride there and back, but I just couldn't focus so I gave up and told myself I'd make up the time somehow because not visiting Dace on the only day she was allowed visitors wasn't an option, especially when she was refusing to see anyone else. And so, for months I would lie in bed with her and we'd watch stupid sitcoms with laugh tracks on Netflix because her therapist said she wasn't allowed to watch *Project Runway* anymore, and then I'd take the bus home, emotionally drained from trying to act like I wasn't as worried as everyone else about her. I spent countless hours staring at my SAT study guides, thinking about Dace instead of prepping.

Eventually, right before Christmas, Crestwood released her. She came back home, declared she was done with modeling, called a truce with her mom and in general seemed to have this new Zen outlook on life. Even though sometimes her mindfulness can be a bit OTT, I try not to roll my eyes at her because the alternative was so much worse.

"I get it—plan B can be A+. But it's not the same thing." I take a sip of my Diet Coke.

Dace just looks at me, dipping her spoon in her yogurt but not actually eating it.

"It's not *exactly* the same thing," I correct myself. "I know you're trying to help, but I can't give up on Tisch."

"I get it, Pippa. It was hard for me too, to give up the dream." Dace fiddles with the cap on her water bottle, her eyes glassy. "Remember The Plan? Our Plan? New York, the two of us? How do you think I felt when that plan was completely taken away from me? My entire life was a setup for what was supposed to come next, once we got out of here. No sports teams so I wouldn't get injured, no clubs so I could go on go-sees . . . all for nothing."

I put my hand on Dace's. "I know. I didn't mean you don't understand."

"I just think you're getting yourself stuck on Tisch, when the other possibilities for you—another college, taking a gap year—they might not be so bad. Look at me, with the trip. It's what's saved me, really. Something to look forward to, and something to help me switch gears, to figure out what my new plan will be. Maybe it's what you need too."

I sigh, not wanting to hurt her feelings by saying that for me, a slacker year is exactly the opposite of what I need. "It's not just me letting myself down if I don't get into Tisch," I say. "It's like I'll be letting my dad down too." I put my head in my hands.

"What're you guys doing over here?" Gemma's standing over our table.

"Plotting to take over the world," Dace says, her tone light.

Gemma puts her hands on her hips. "I don't like the sounds of that."

"You wouldn't. I feel like I'm coming down with a cold, so I convinced Pip to sit alone with me so that I only infect her, not the entire student body a month before EVERYTHING."

Gemma takes a step back. "Ick. Thanks for the warning. Nothing is keeping me from Senior Sleepover," she says as though it's completely plausible that she'll catch a cold in April and be down for the count in May. But Gemma's always been a bit of a hypochondriac. While prom is of course a big deal at Spalding High, Senior Sleepover is an even bigger event, maybe because it doesn't feel overdone. Like, every high school has prom. Who's ever heard of Senior Sleepover? No one, except those of us who go to Spalding, where we all claim the concept of Senior Sleepover was invented. Anyway, what it is: it happens in mid-May, on the final Thursday before exams start, and all the seniors sleep over on the football field. Everyone has a theme to their PJ look—Holly Golightly from *Breakfast at Tiffany's* is always a big one (white shirtdress, sleep mask and tassel earrings)—and it seems like everyone talks and preps for Senior Sleepover way more than prom. Also there's status with Senior Sleepover because after you stay up all night, everyone goes out for breakfast at the Orange Turtle, and then you go back to school and hang out all day, not going to class, while all the freshman, sophomores and juniors get all jealous that they're not seniors yet.

As Gemma heads back to the table where we usually sit, I turn back to Dace. "Thanks for covering."

"Don't mention it." She fiddles with the Hamsa around her neck, this small pewter palm-shaped charm she wears now that's supposed to bring her happiness and good luck. "OK, speaking of Senior Sleepover, I think we need to lock down a date to PJ shop before we're left with bargain-bin dregs. How's Thursday after school?"

"Sure. Though I still have zero inspo. Maybe we should just do *Grease* after all?"

Dace slams her hands on the table. "No way. We can do better."

Annie, Gemma and Emma asked us to do the *Grease* sleepover: Sandra Dee, Rizzo, Jan, Frenchy and Marty, but Dace doesn't want to because every year some girls re-enact the *Grease* sleepover for Senior Sleepover, so it's kind of super-unoriginal, plus there's talk that a bunch of girls on the field hockey team are going as *Grease* too.

"I really want to do something that's just the two of us. Just in case you end up going to prom, like, with a date." Dace used to go out with about five guys at a time, but ever since she got back from Crestwood, she's laid pretty low on the guy front. She says she's focusing on herself instead.

"Yeah, with all those boys dying to go out with me. I bet I end up going alone."

"Hundred percent, with that attitude."

"I'm being real. I haven't had any action since October, with that unfortunate makeout session with Pablo."

"Pablo with the good hair. So what if his braces cut your lip? Anyway, I was thinking more like some other guys. Ben, Dylan . . ."

My heartbeat speeds up. Whoever said distance makes the heart grow fonder was on to something. As much as I've tried to forget Dylan, I think about him a lot. After our break-up, Dylan and I ran into each other at Spalding's 50th anniversary. He was with Muse, and it was super awkward. And the next day Dace found my lost phone, and he had texted, saying he hoped we could still be friends. I never replied, mostly because I didn't want to be friends with someone who had ripped my heart out and then shoved it in his garbage disposal. And then a day passed, then a week, and then so much time that it would be weird to even reply. So I didn't.

"Dylan probably has some super-cute Harvard girlfriend by now," I tell Dace.

"Interesting that you focused on Dylan. I thought Ben told you he'd be back this week." Unlike Dylan and I, Ben and I actually stayed friends this year, while he was in Park City.

"Ben and I are *just friends*. You know that."

"Who says you can't go to prom with a friend? Especially when that friend is inarguably good-looking and will make for really good prom pics," Dace challenges.

"It took Ben and I long enough to get to a comfortable platonic stage. I don't want to mess with that. Besides, he's not going to want to go to prom. He just went last year."

"Well, I know someone who didn't go to prom last year. Or at all, technically. If that's your main criteria."

As I pop my last fry in my mouth, my thoughts go straight to that person: Dylan McCutter.

•   •   •

I'm sitting in Writer's Craft, stumped by today's exercise—a short story with the theme of Escape—when I get called down to the guidance counselor's office. Mr. Aquila's door is open, and he smiles at me when I walk in—though it's one of those upside-down smiles, the kind where the person is actually frowning.

"Pippa," he says, gesturing to the chair in front of him.

"Hi," I say, sitting down.

My stomach feels like it's full of marbles. He's going to mention Tisch. I just know it. Of course the guidance counselor knows all about who's accepted and rejected and *waitlisted* to every college. I wonder if it would be awkward to bolt from the room? There's an escape idea for my short story assignment.

"So I was checking your file, and I noticed that you're short community service hours this year."

"I *am*?" I lean forward in my chair and peer at his file. It definitely says *GREENE, PHILADELPHIA* across the top.

"I've got the hospital hours here, but you need ten more hours to graduate."

"That can't be right. I spent hours and hours there. Like *waaaay* more than I needed to."

Mr. Aquila nods. "I think that's where the mix-up occurred. It may be that you filled more than the required hours, but there's a loophole in that"—he reads from the paper in front of him—"a percentage of the hours have to be completed in the school year in which the student graduates."

Noooooooooo . . . It's probably very bad karma to think negative thoughts about a good deed, but I can't stop the dread.

Mr. Bad News blathers on. "There aren't a lot of open spots left at this point, especially for a shorter commitment. The hospital's program is full. How do you feel about keeping our earth green?"

"Is that code for picking up garbage?"

"You're quick." He grins. "Part of the Hanlan's Field grounds are owned by the town; they need someone to pick up garbage left outside the concert facility after events."

Well, this isn't *that* bad. "So I can see concerts for free?"

"Not exactly. The school's rules say you can't complete volunteer hours after 9 p.m., for safety and liability reasons. And the city wants the area clean before 9 a.m., which means you'll need to go the morning after a concert. The estimated time is an hour. So you could do it ten times and be done." He hands me a piece of paper with a calendar of concerts as well as what look like guidelines on how to pick up garbage.

Amazing. Just how I want to be spending my mornings.

"Oh, and Pippa? We get updates about college acceptances, rejections, that sort of thing." He pauses. "I was sorry to hear about Tisch. I can only imagine how you must be feeling."

"Thanks," I say, my cheeks burning. For a moment it's hard to talk. "Do you—do you know what I could do to get off the waitlist?"

Mr. Aquila presses his lips together and shakes his head. "You know, we've never had anyone go to Tisch before. I'm just not even sure how to counsel you on this one. Is there any advice on their website?"

I shake my head. "I'm supposed to confirm that I want to be on the waitlist. I haven't done it yet because I was hoping there might be some way around it."

Mr. Aquila puts my file away. "Hmm. I know you felt fairly strongly about not applying to other colleges, but I could help you look into which colleges are still accepting late applications, if you like."

I shake my head. "No thanks. I'll just figure this out." Then I stand and trudge out of his office, closing the door behind me.

●　●　●

I head home after my *Hall Pass* meeting, expecting to find the house empty since Mom always works late on Tuesdays, but Hank's car is in the driveway. And when I open the door, there's a huge shiny silver helium balloon that says *Congratulations!* in bright rainbow font. My stomach sinks. Somewhere, over some rainbow, someone deserves this balloon, but it's not me. Mom rushes to greet me, and as she's hugging me I see a mop of curly blond hair flying in the air through the kitchen window. Charley's bouncing on a mini trampoline in the backyard. Of course he's here: everywhere Hank goes, Charley goes. Hank's ex-wife still lives in Columbus, where she does shift work at a hospital. Hank has custody of Charley throughout the school year and then Charley spends holidays and summer vacation with his mom. I am not Charley's biggest fan. He's cute, but also eight years old. Obsessed with burps, farts and professional wrestling. I started counting down to summer vacation the day Charley got back from Columbus.

Right now, though, I couldn't be more relieved to see the kid. Or Hank, who rounds the corner from the kitchen. Their presence is the perfect excuse not to tell Mom the truth. That conversation is for Greenes only.

"Why aren't you at work?" I ask Mom.

"Are you kidding? I switched shifts so I could be here to celebrate! My only daughter getting into her first-choice college doesn't happen every day!"

The tile floor feels like quicksand. I'm sinking, sinking, sinking.

Mom takes my hand and pulls me along to the kitchen, where there are more balloons and a cake that says *Tisch* ♥s *Pippa*, and for a split second, it feels real. But then I remember that actually Tisch does not heart me at all.

"Oh honey," Mom gushes. "I picked up a bottle of prosecco. I figured it was a special occasion and you could have a tiny glass," she says, giddy.

Hank pats me on the back, awkwardly. I force a smile and wonder if there's any way that Hank might know I got waitlisted. Could Aquila have told him over burnt coffee in the staffroom?

"Now tell us everything," Mom says, pulling out a chair for me to sit down. I slump into the chair and force myself not to slam my forehead into the wood surface of the table. Too bad I didn't apply to the drama program instead.

At 6:04 a.m. I get an idea.

"Who died?" David grumbles into the phone when he answers.

"What? No one died. That's super morbid."

"What time is it?"

"6:07. Good morning."

"Not morning, Greene. Not when you go to bed at two, and for the record, no one should be called this early unless someone died."

"OK, OK, sorry, but I've got a crisis."

"Are you OK?" David's voice changes into Serious Dad Tone, something I've heard only twice since he was officially outed as Bio Dad. "Your mom?"

"We're both fine. I mean, I assume she's fine. She's working the overnight shift, saving one animal's life at a time. Anyway, it's not *that* kind of crisis, but it's still important and you're the only one who can help me."

He yawns loudly. "Well, when you put it that way. Let me make some coffee." I hear shuffling and I picture David climbing down the ladder from his loft bed to the main floor of his photo studio, his bare feet on the concrete flooring, slipping into his lambswool slippers, the ones he always leaves at the base of the ladder before climbing into bed. David has a thing for slippers. On my last birthday, he sent me a pair of slippers, and then told me he had an identical pair at his place for when I'm in New York.

What if I never have a reason to go to New York again?

There's a lot of clanging happening on the other end of the line and then David clears his throat. "We're in business. All right, what's up?"

"Tisch waitlisted me."

"Waitlisted? Oh shit. Sorry. Shoot. You sure?"

"Yeah. I don't think there's any mistaking when they say 'unfortunately' in the email. And I didn't apply to any other schools but I told Mom I did and she also thinks I got into Tisch and there are balloons everywhere and I've got to talk to the program director, Mr. Vishwanathan, about this and convince him to let me in. But I don't know his number."

I half expect David to tell me that maybe getting waitlisted is a sign, that I have to put my college eggs in other college baskets, but instead he says, "I know Amir." After a beat he adds, "Vishwanathan."

"You *know* him?"

"Yeah. We went to Tisch together. He's the one who bugs me to be a mentor every year. I'll give him a call. But I'm going to wait until the sun rises. So you should probably go eat something. Or go shoot the sunrise. No better way to start your day than catching the golden hour."

Relief washes over me. "Thanks, David. You're the best."

"Don't thank me yet. Oh, and Greene?"

"Yeah?"

David yawns loudly. "Tell your mother."

● ◍ ◉

Hanlan's Field is two long bus rides away from my house, reinforcing my dire need for a license. The storage shed where I'm supposed to pick up my supplies is off to the left of the entrance and the combination lock takes me three tries with a set of numbers Mr. Aquila gave me. The plastic doors of the shed squeak open to a musty interior. I pull out the gloves, garbage bag and garbage picking stick, then close up the shed and make my up way up the grassy hill. The same grassy hill where Dylan and I saw the Cherry Blasters. What a great moment that was. This moment? Not so great. I jab the metal poker into a beer cup and push the poker into the trash bag, but the beer cup won't come off. I have to actually pull the cup off the poker. Every time. Poker. Beer cup. Trash bag. Pull. Poker. Beer cup. Trash bag. Pull. How hard is it to throw your empties in the trash? I resolve to always throw my garbage away, no matter what. I should be good at it. I've already thrown away my future as a photographer, why not everything else?

Whoa.

OK.

Rein it in, Pip.

I do the exercise Dr. Judy taught me to redirect my thinking when it goes off the rails. I close my eyes, then open them and focus on my surroundings instead. The sun is peeking through the branches of the trees, the sky reddish-pink, the shadows long, creating leading lines across the grass. I grab my camera from my bag and move around, working angles to get the best shot.

Flipping through the frames on the screen, I decide David was right. There is no better way to start the day than with your camera and the golden hour. Even if it means having to pick up garbage.

Dace and I are walking to her car after school when I feel my phone vibrate in the back pocket of my jeans. I whip it out.

> David: Noon tomorrow. Vishwanathan's office. You've got 15 minutes with him. Can you do it?

My hands shake.

> Me: Yes.

I turn to Dace and show her the texts.
"Christ the Redeemer!"
I give her a look.
"Famous statue in Rio. Anyway! Not important! The meeting. Tomorrow. In Manhattan?"

I stare at my phone then back at her and nod. "I guess? What am I going to say? How am I going to get there? What am I going to tell my mom? I can't go PJ shopping. I'm sorry."

"Forget shopping. This is your life." She clicks her fob and the car unlocks. "Get in. I'm driving you home, and then I'll pack for you while you figure out what to say to this dude. Then when you're ready I'll pretend to be him and you can practice on me."

"You don't have to."

"Get in." She gets into the driver's side, and I open the passenger door and slide in. I turn to face her as she starts up the car. "You were there for me night and day last year. Now it's my turn." Dace cranks the music and heads out of the parking lot onto Elm Street.

A billion emotions run through me—anticipation, excitement, worry, fear. And one nagging voice that asks how I'm going to explain to Mom that I suddenly need to go to New York.

•   •   •

Long after Dace and I have rehearsed what I'm going to say, packed, bought my return bus ticket and Dace has gone home, Mom arrives home from work. "Worked a double," she says, as she kicks off her shoes and trudges into the kitchen. Dark circles sit under her eyes, and she looks about five years older than she did this morning. I follow her and open my mouth, prepared to blurt out the truth about the whole waitlisting thing, but instead something about a pre-orientation orientation comes out, which doesn't make any sense whatsoever, but it's so far-fetched and she's so tired that Mom just nods, taking it in.

"Oh OK," she says slowly. "But tomorrow? I just don't see how they expect students to come on such short notice."

"I think it's probably my fault. I hadn't checked my emails in a few days. But I really want to go. And I'd just be missing one day of school. I checked the bus schedule, and there's a bus that leaves at 9 tonight. I already called Aunt Emmy and she said I could stay with her tomorrow night and I'd come home on Saturday."

"Wow. It sounds like you really want to do this. But the overnight bus? Is there anything in the morning?"

"Nothing that will guarantee I make it to the meet—er, pre-orientation on time."

She rubs her forehead. "All right."

Mom turns on the kitchen faucet and fills a glass with water. She takes a sip then puts her glass down on the counter. "And does it cost anything, aside from the bus ticket?"

I shake my head and fiddle with a stack of papers on the table, trying to figure out if Mom's going to agree or not. She takes another sip of her water.

"I guess you should do it. You'll probably get a chance to meet some of your classmates and instructors right? That will be nice." She puts her glass in the sink, then turns back to me. "Do you think you'll have a chance to talk to anyone about possible scholarships? I know they didn't offer you one with admission, but maybe there are others you can apply for now that you've been accepted? Of course I'll make it work no matter what, but if there's free money to be had . . ."

My gut feels like it's slowly descending down my legs to my toes. It's only now dawning on me that ever since I told her I got in, she's been worrying about how we're going to pay for Tisch. Which is probably why she took the double shift today.

There's a second where it feels like it's all too much. My mouth opens. The truth is there, right around my larynx. That's where it stays, though.

Maybe if I can just convince Vishwanathan to let me in, my lie won't actually be a lie but the truth. I just have to hold it together.

●   ●   ●

"Try to get your own seat, don't talk to anyone weird and take a cab from the bus station—and text me when you get there. OK?" Mom says as we stand outside the bus, my overnight bag in hand. For a second the look she gives me, it's like she's going to cry. She hugs me, and then I lug my bag up the four wide steps and onto the bus. I settle into a seat near the back and reach into my backpack to pull out my headphones. My fingers feel something smooth, and I pull out a small envelope with my name on the front, in Dace's loopy handwriting. Under it she's written *You got this.* I run my finger under the flap of the envelope to open it and then I pull out Dace's

Hamsa, the palm-shaped charm she wears around her neck. I could use the good luck and happiness. I squeeze it tight and mentally run through what I plan to say to Vishwanathan a few more times, until my words are running together, and my eyelids are too heavy. I push the Hamsa into my jeans pocket, lean against the window and close my eyes.

The bus pulls into the station and I'm up. I sling my bag over my shoulder and follow the single file of people off the bus and in through the grimy glass doors of the Port Authority terminal. Fluorescent lighting makes the terminal look like it could be any time of day. A vending machine with a lone bag of chips takes up valuable space as people rush in each direction, a human Chinese checkers board. I make my way in as straight a line as possible to the stairs; a mix of burnt coffee, oil and sweat fills the air. At the exit, I push the doors hard through the wind tunnel that's created in the entrance to the station. Outside is another wave of smells: gasoline, but also the smell of spring—flowers and leaves—and it fills me with a vague sense of hope. I look down 8th Avenue to see where the line for cabs starts.

"Need a lift, Greene?"

I turn and there's David. Hands in the pockets of his brown leather jacket, driving cap pulled down to his eyebrows, three-day stubble on his chin. He winks.

"David!" I drop my bag and hug him. "You didn't have to come up here," I say, but I'm so glad he did.

"Well you gave me your bus information . . ." His voice is teasing. "And I didn't have anything better to do this morning at 6 a.m.," he says. He picks up my bag. "Geez. How long are you staying?" he says, hefting its weight.

"I need outfit options. I want to make a good impression," I say.

"All right, all right, come on."

We climb into a yellow cab and it cuts across 42nd and then turns south onto 11th Avenue. The cab zips past bikers and leafy trees, dog walkers and brownstones. It's early, but this city is so full of life. Just a few days ago, I'd been thinking of this moment, when I returned to New York, but I thought it would be at the end of August, when I was moving into the dorms, ready to start the first of my four years at Tisch. Never did I anticipate I'd be here now, on a desperate last-ditch attempt just to get in.

"Perfect light for shooting," David says as the cab merges onto the West Side Highway. He's right. The sun is just starting to crest over the horizon, casting a golden glow on the skyscrapers. Life looks more promising during the golden hour. Pure, unblemished. I grab my camera from my bag and roll down my window, then point my camera across the water toward Hoboken and snap a few shots, trying to immerse myself in the tiny rectangle of view. I make a mental note to save the shot for next week's Insta. I'll do gold as my color theme now that I have this shot and the sunrise shot from Hanlan's.

We pull up in front of Emmy's house, and David pays the driver as I slide out. David's studio faces Christopher Street, kitty-corner to the apartment where my Aunt Emmy lives, which also happens to be where my parents lived in New York. Well, my real dad and mom. I mean, the dad who raised me. Not David. Oh, it's complicated.

"I'll wait here while you make sure she's up," David says.

The apartment building's front steps are pitted, the black paint on them chipping off, and the door's red paint is too. I run my fingers over the name plates—from top to bottom—and then push the button by *E. Greene*. Dad's name. Typed with a type-writer on a slip of paper that's got to be more than 18 years old at this point.

I always imagine myself in a sort of *Back to the Future* scenario, me in the same world as my mom and dad when they lived in New York. When Dad was sharing a studio with David, that summer when they met my mom. I'd be the friend who made sure my mom and dad hooked up, instead of Mom and David getting together first and Mom getting preg-nant with me.

Whenever I share this time-traveling fantasy aloud though, Dace reminds me I wouldn't be *me* if David and Mom hadn't gotten together. If David wasn't my biological father. He stayed in the background, letting Evan be my dad, until my dad died. Until the whole complicated truth came out. It would be easy for me to stay mad at David for the rest of my life, but he has become kind of like an uncle to me since Dad died. He wasn't a part of my life for so many years, but these days, when it matters, he's there for me.

A moment later there's a buzz and the door clicks. I push it open, then turn to wave bye to David. He gives me a salute and then turns to head down Christopher, and I walk down the long narrow hallway, past the rows of metal mailboxes on the left, and then past the bright blue door of the elevator that's been out of service for years. I take the stairs two at a time to the second floor. I'm about to rap on the door to apartment 2D when Emmy pulls it open. I turn my ready-to-knock fist into a wave and she pulls me in for a bear hug.

●　●　●

The Tisch building is fronted by glass windows with displays showcasing students' work. Every time I see the displays (or whenever I dream about being here), I envision one of my photographs in there, blown up. The handful of students in the foyer look me over without comment. Up on the fourth floor, the first thing you see is a wall of Polaroids of all the instructors, with arrows in Sharpies pointing the way to their offices. Vishwanathan's photo is at the end. I make my way down the hallway and knock on 405.

The door opens silently.

"Ms. Greene?" Mr. Vishwanathan is standing in front of me. He's tall and lanky, with a wiry salt-and-pepper beard and clear-framed glasses.

He holds the door open for me and ushers me into a large, industrial office: slate floor, concrete walls covered in large black-and-white photographs, some framed prints, some canvas prints. Streetscapes of New York, San Francisco and other places I don't recognize. Are they all his work?

Vishwanathan clears his throat and I realize I've been standing in the middle of the office, taking it in. He's already seated behind a large mahogany desk, leaning forward. Looking at me expectantly. He points to the chair on the other side of the desk, which I'm relieved to take given how shaky my legs suddenly are.

"Thank you so much for meeting with me," I blurt then sit down.

He leans back in his chair and folds his hands together. "David asked me to meet with you." He pauses and I take it as my cue to dive in.

"Um, yes. I was hoping to talk to you about coming here. I was waitlisted."

He nods. "Right. We don't typically meet with applicants, but David and I go way back."

I can't tell from his tone whether or not that means he and David are friends. "I had a chance to look at your file," he says, swiveling his computer monitor so that I can see that he is, in fact, looking at my file. "You came to Tisch camp your junior year."

"Yes," I say, relieved for this starting-off point. Surely they don't turn away students they already saw fit for their camp. "It was fantastic. I loved every minute of it. I've wanted to go to Tisch my entire life."

"You and everyone else who applies," he says lightly, clicking around on his screen.

I close my eyes for a moment, remembering the pitch I practiced. "I've definitely broadened my range because of the Tisch camp. When I first starting taking photography seriously, when I was, like, 15, my goal was to shoot fashion. My best friend was a model, and we had this whole plan that we'd move to New York together—her to model, me to be the photographer. We kind of thought she could just choose her photographer." I laugh nervously. "But after my dad died, I don't know, I guess I started to think about things—life—in a different way. I started exploring other types of photography. More realistic portraiture. The unexpected, the unposed, the unpolished. Shooting fashion was perfection captured, but shooting life became, to me, capturing perfection."

Mr. Vishwanathan nods. We're both quiet for a moment. I open my mouth to talk, just to fill the silence, but then he leans forward in his leather chair. "Why don't you tell me about yourself."

"Oh, um, OK." Tell him about myself? I kind of feel like I just did. "Well . . ." I grip my knees and think back to what I wrote in my application essay. I want to be consistent in my answer. Maybe this is a test to see if I actually wrote my own essay? "I'm a senior—obviously. I've always wanted to be a photographer. My dad was a photographer so I was exposed to life behind the lens from a very young age. I got my first camera when I was five," I say, smiling, hoping he'll smile back. He doesn't. I clear my throat. "I have three cameras, and I'm thinking about getting a new 50 mm lens. I take pictures of everything. All day, every day. It's the way I see the world."

Vishwanathan holds up his hand. "Please stop."

"Um, sorry?" I look behind me, hoping someone's just come into his office. Not that he doesn't like what I'm saying. But there's no one behind me. I turn back to him.

"I asked you to tell me about *yourself*. So far you've described everyone who applies to the program. What I want to know is what sets you apart? What are your interests *outside* photography?"

"Oh, well, um. I'm on the school paper staff—"

"Photo editor?

"Yes," I say proudly, wondering if he remembers reading that on my application. "Oh and I was yearbook editor last year. And founder of our school's photo club."

"All photography."

"Well, yes, but—"

"Ms. Greene, do you realize how many thousands of applicants we get for this program?"

I take a wild guess. "Five thousand?"

"You're not far off. Do you know what proportion were photo editor on their school newspaper or website?"

This time I don't guess. This time I just shake my head.

"More than 75 percent. What else do you do that's not photography? Any other clubs?"

What else? What does he want me to say? That I'm in the Muggles Club? (We actually do have one but I've never been able to get into Harry Potter. Sue me.) "Oh! Ski club. I did that junior year."

"But not this year? It was a great winter for snow upstate, wasn't it?"

"Yes, but I really wanted to make sure my grades were good and with studying for SATs it felt irresponsible to be out late on a Friday night and then wake up late on a Saturday morning."

He raises his eyebrows as though I've just said I thought it was important to smoke weed every Friday night. "What about a job?"

"Well, no, not this year. I did volunteer in my junior year at the local hospital though."

"For the required hours to graduate?"

I nod. Who on earth has time to do volunteer hours for fun?

"And how did you enjoy that?"

My mind goes straight to Dylan, and I can feel my face getting hot. "It was, um, great."

"All right." Vishwanathan picks up his phone, looks at it and places it face down on the desk. Am I running out of time? "Tell me, Pippa, is there anything else that you think we should know about you as a candidate?"

I take a deep breath. I purposely didn't mention that David and my dad went to Tisch in my application, because I wanted to get in based on my own merits. Not because of the so-called legacy preference that is rumored to exist at a lot of colleges. But I'm feeling desperate. "I'm not sure if you know, but David Westerly is my biological father. And the father I was raised by is Evan Greene. Both are Tisch alumni. I'm not sure if you remember Evan too? Maybe you were all in the same class or something? Evan and David were best friends and roommates." I try to read Vishwanathan's face for any clue that what I'm saying is making any difference whatsoever, but he seems to have about as much emotion as an avocado. "Anyway, I look up to both of them so much. It feels like it's in my blood, you know?" There. I've said it.

Vishwanathan leans forward in his chair. "Well, that's certainly interesting. And we do love to see the passion for photography passed down, but of course we do not give any preference to legacy students. I'm sure you can see how that would be unfair to other applicants."

My back feels sweaty. "Of course, I didn't mean . . . I just meant that I've known about Tisch forever." We stare at each other. I clear my throat. "Mr. Vishwanathan, I'm really, really grateful for this meeting and I came all the way here for it, on a bus, overnight, and it was to tell you that I have to—I need to—go to Tisch. I will seriously do *anything* it takes. If you'll just tell me what you're looking for, what I didn't do that you were hoping I would, I'll do it. I'll rewrite my essay. I'll change my portfolio.

I'll show you whatever you want to see. Maybe I just didn't understand what you were looking for."

He clasps his hands in front of him. "Actually, Pippa, I think that's precisely your problem. It feels as though you're so focused on getting in that you're trying to give us what we want. When what we want is to see what makes you who you are. It's your interests, your passions, your inspiration that make you a better photographer. Do you understand what I'm saying?"

I nod numbly. But I don't get it. My interests, my passions, my inspiration? It's being a photographer. Taking pictures. Getting that great shot. It's a photography program. How can I be so off the mark?

He stands, and then I realize that's my cue. He's kicking me out. He opens the door, then turns to me.

"Expand your experiences, Ms. Greene. Push yourself outside your comfort zone. Try things you normally wouldn't. Take a stand for something. Join a sports club. Learn a new skill. Don't just take pictures. In fact, *don't* take pictures. Leave your camera at home and really live. Don't be afraid to fail. That's what we want to see."

They want to see applicants failing? How about failing to get into their dream college? How can I show him that?

He puts a hand on the door. "You have the opportunity to submit a 500-word essay by May 18. The admissions committee reviews all essays and chooses the best candidates to fill any open spots. That is, should there be any openings available. You may not want to take that chance. Perhaps you will consider accepting an offer from one of the other colleges you applied to."

Right. One of the other colleges I applied to. I stick out my hand to shake Mr. Vishwanathan's, thank him for his time, and shuffle out the door.

"Oh, and Ms. Greene?" I turn. "Enjoy the rest of your time in the city."

Yeah, I'll get right on that.

●　●　●

Outside, the cherry blossoms are in full bloom, lining the street in clouds of pinks and purples, perfect for my Instagram post this week, but now I can't really focus on anything through my tears. And even if I could, I'm not supposed to take pictures? I'm supposed to . . . what? Climb the tree and break out in song? Or grab a stack of tissue paper and rec-reate cherry blossoms using Elmer's glue?

I should probably let Aunt Emmy or David know I'm out of the meeting, but I can't bring myself to rehash it all just yet, or deal with the guilt I'm feeling that they know what's really going on when Mom's still in the dark, thinking I'm in pre-orientation orien-tation land. I can't bear to tell any of them that the meeting, and that coming to New York, was com-pletely, utterly, hopelessly pointless. I walk through Washington Square Park and make my way over to an empty bench by the fountain. The sun shining down feels like it's mocking me. Hey, cheerful sun, guess what? You suck. Just like everything else in the world.

I stare at the fountain in front of me and watch as a little girl, maybe four or five, walks closer to the water, holding her mother's hand. The mother leans down and hands her a coin, the sun glinting off it. The girl winds up and then hurls the coin into the fountain. I wonder what she wished for and try to remember when I was that young. When I believed that your wishes could come true simply by tossing a coin in a fountain. I close my eyes just as my phone dings.

Ramona: Almost there.

I forgot I'd texted Ramona last night from the bus to see if she wanted to meet up after my meeting. I'm supposed to be at Think, this coffee shop on Mercer at West 3rd, in five minutes. I make my way back through the park to West 4th. I didn't tell Ramona why I was coming to the city, because about 87 percent of me believed that when we met up, we'd be celebrating over five-dollar coffees that I got into the program, like her. Ramona got early acceptance to Tisch back in the fall.

"Pippa!" I look up to see Ramona waving at me from the steps in front of Think.

She bounds down the steps, her bright red curls flying everywhere. "I'm so excited to see you!" She chatters away as we walk in. We place our orders and then get our coffees at the other end of the bar. It's not until we're sitting that she asks why I'm in town. "How long are you here for? Who did you come with? Tell me everything."

I take a sip of my latte, tears welling up in my eyes. I place my mug back down on the wood table. "I got waitlisted."

Ramona's jaw drops as she leans forward, slapping her hands on the table. "Shut. Up. You're kidding."

I shake my head.

"I don't understand. Your stuff is amazing. Did they tell you why?"

"Uh uh." I tell her about David getting me a meeting with Vishwanathan, and how I'm supposed to show him how I'm *not* taking photos to get into a photography program. "The worst part is that now I have to go home to my mom and tell her that there's a really good chance I'm not going to get into Tisch and that I have no backup plan."

"Yikes. But wait: you already told her you got in, and she bought it, and she thinks you're here because you got in, right?"

I nod, staring into my coffee cup.

Ramona claps her hands together and I look up. "And you still *want* to go to Tisch, obvs. And there's still a chance you will; you just have to, like, expand your horizons or whatever. Which, how hard could that be? Point is, if your mom already thinks you're going to Tisch, then why bother telling her anything at this point? Why not just *make sure* you get in? And you're here, right? In the most fun city in the world, and you've got an entire parent-free afternoon and night. Sounds like the perfect recipe to start doing some of those wild and crazy things Vishwanathan wants you to be doing."

"He didn't say *wild and crazy*."

Ramona waves a hand at me. "Text your mom and your aunt and David and whoever else you need to. Tell them that everything is awesome and you're hanging out with me for the rest of the day. Go on."

I bite my lip and then pick up my phone. I pause for a second, and text Emmy first, then David, then Mom. Then look back to Ramona. "OK. Now what?"

"Now? Now we have some fun."

● ● ●

Eight hours later we're standing at a street corner in Chelsea waiting for the light to change. We cross the street toward a lineup of twentysomethings in hipster variations on T-shirts and jeans.

"Who were you supposed to come with again?" I ask Ramona as we join the line. An hour ago over pizza and Cokes, after an afternoon of deliberate non-photography activities—shopping (her) and window shopping (me), the Central Park zoo, the Guggenheim, 10-dollar manicures, green smoothies, a visit to the Strand (where Ramona had to steer me clear of the photography books and into the stationery section)—she told me Ryder & Chase had a show tonight. I'd already texted Emmy to ask if it was OK if I got to her place around midnight, having assumed that Ramona meant she had two tickets to the concert and wanted to give me one of them.

"Hmm?" she says now.

"The extra ticket. Whose was it?"

"Riiiiiight. About that. There's just one teensy

tiny catch," she says. Ramona smiles a smile I haven't seen in a while. "It's a sold-out show—plus it's 21 and over. And my fake ID is on backorder or something, and I'm guessing you don't have a fake driver's license . . ."

"I don't even have a real driver's license."

"So we're going to have to sneak in."

"Um, what?" I whisper. I shake my head. "On top of everything, I really don't need to get arrested."

She laughs. "Think of it as a challenge. Have you ever snuck into a concert before?"

"No."

"See? You're expanding your horizons. Yet another non-photography experience to add to your day. You're welcome"

"I'm not sure this is what Vishwanathan had in mind."

"Come on, it'll be fun." She grabs my hand, and we move away from the line to the side of the building and down an alley.

"What are we doing?"

She sees my skeptical look and shrugs. "If everyone else is going in the front, then we better go around to the back. The band's got to get in some way, right?"

"I think I'm having a panic attack," I venture. "Yeah—"

"Nice try. It's called an adrenaline rush. It's because you're *excited* at the prospect of doing something *exciting*," Ramona whispers. "C'mon."

The alley is dark. But when we make it through to the back, a black tour bus is parked a few feet away, with a couple of other cars parked beside it on the gravel lot. We come to a black metal door, but it's one of the ones that doesn't have a handle on the outside. Ramona twirls a curl. "OK. Let's hang out here until the door opens. Then we just walk in. Calmly, like no big deal, but, like, quick enough that we can catch the door before it shuts."

We wait. The longer we stand there, the more nervous I get.

"Why don't we just go to a movie?" I ask, just as the door opens and a guy—tall, skinny, jeans sliding down his butt—emerges. Scratchy guitars mix with a heavy drum beat—the opener must already be on stage. Ramona grabs the door, turns to check that I'm right behind her and then we slip inside. The guy barely glances over as he puts a cigarette in his mouth. I press as close to Ramona as I can. We step into the hallway and let the door close behind us. And grin. Could it really be so easy?

"Not so fast." This guy looms over us. He's burly, hairy, all in black, clothes a size too small. I look up at his face with its deep lines and slowly back away. He blocks the hallway with one big arm. The bouncer could crush us both with one hand.

"Pippa?" I turn around to see who could possibly be calling my name. Dark brown hair sweeps over the top of his head, hanging just long enough to tuck behind his ears. His face is chiseled, his cheekbones jutting out more than I remember. That dimple. And those green eyes that are locked with mine.

Dylan McCutter. He shoves a box toward me and I grab it. "You guys are *so* late. Come on!" His eyes are wide. "Sorry about that," Dylan says to the bouncer. "I guess they got locked out."

The bouncer looks past us, already disinterested, and lets his arm drop.

We follow Dylan down the long dark hallway to the merch booth, where he unlocks the door and holds it open for us, taking the box back from me and giving me an amused smile. I open my mouth, unsure where to start.

Thank you.

You saved us.

What are you doing here?

You're so hot.

He shakes his head. "Philadelphia Greene." He sets the box down on a bunch of others on the floor, then points to a large cashbox under the counter. "Cashbox's under the counter. Prices on the wall. You—" He nods at Ramona.

"Ramona," she says, wide eyed.

"You write down the order in the notebook." He slaps a notebook at Ramona's chest.

"Um, OK?" Ramona says, looking at me.

I let my eyes run over him—his hair is longer, his face older, more angular, his shoulders broader, and the Ryder & Chase T-shirt he's wearing is tight on his upper arms. Swoon.

"Hey, thanks," I say, my voice catching.

"If we can get through this line before the band goes on, I'll be thanking you. I'm understaffed tonight. All right, let's get at it." He nods to the guy in line who's holding a twenty.

"Finally. Gray T-shirt with the logo." He points at the wall behind our heads.

"Gray T-shirt with the logo!" I shout.

"Size!" Dylan hollers back.

"Eek right! What size?"

"Large."

I look at the price on the bright yellow cardboard starburst pinned to the shirt on the wall and turn back to him. "Twenty dollars."

He hands me the crumpled bill as Dylan tosses the shirt to me.

I fiddle with the cashbox but it won't open. Ramona's scrambling around the floor, yelling that she's dropped her pen and people are barking orders and I want to crawl under the counter and hide from this insanity. But then Dylan's crouching beside me, popping open the cashbox and our eyes meet and then he helps me back up and I'm taking the next order, and minutes later, I'm in a groove. We're doing it. Selling the stuff. It's so fast-paced I barely—*barely*—have time to think about what is going on. I'm in New York, at a concert I snuck into, selling T-shirts with Dylan McCutter. I wipe my palms, which are hot and sweaty, on my jeans, glad I wore a cute outfit. Even if it is all black.

Eventually the line clears and Dylan comes over to stand near me, his back against the wall. He kicks the toe of my shoe with his. "Whew. You did it. That was impressive."

"And intense."

"Yeah." He grins as Ramona comes over to stand

near us. "I'm Dylan, by the way. I guess I forgot to mention that."

Ramona presses her lips together and looks from Dylan to me, and I know what she's thinking because she knows *everything* there is to know about Dylan. From when we were together until when we broke up, and that epic text that I never replied to.

"So . . . what are you doing here?" Dylan says, his eyes twinkling. I try to remind myself that his eyes *always* twinkle. They're twinkly eyes. That's it. They're not twinkling for *me*.

"I always wanted to sell T-shirts?" I fiddle with the handle on the cashbox.

"Living the dream."

I smile. "Actually, Ramona invited me to the show. She just *forgot* to tell me that we didn't have tickets."

He laughs.

"Luckily I know that deep down Pippa is wild and crazy." Ramona hops over the counter, hollering that she's going to the washroom.

Dylan turns back to me. "Wild and crazy?"

"Long story."

"So what are you doing here, in New York?"

"I had this thing at Tisch—"

"So you got in. Of course you got in. Seriously, what can't you do?"

"Actually . . ." I say, trying to get the truth out. But Dylan's grabbing my shoulders and pulling me in for a hug.

"Come here." His arms are around me and he feels so good and everything seems to stop—except my pounding heart, which I'm pretty sure Dylan can feel through my chest. Finally we pull apart. "Way to go." He slaps me on the shoulder, like I'm his frat brother.

I clear my throat. "So, um, what about you?"

"Me? Harvard. The music program. And remember JJ? He's at Boston College and Sig's at UMass, so we've kind of gotten the band back together and are taking it mildly seriously. Setting up a few shows for the summer. I could let you know, if you're around. If you wanna come sometime."

I would love to see Dylan's band but as if I'm just going to *be around* New York City. "Wow. So you guys are here for the summer? In New York?" I say.

"Nah. I'm just here for the week to work for my uncle. It'd be cool to stay the summer, but I've got to save up for school. I'll be working the merch booth at Hanlan's. It's a Spalding summer for me."

My heart is racing. Dylan is moving back to Spalding. Which, OK, I know it's not because of me. But for the first time in days, I feel genuinely excited about something. Then I remember this is our first conversation in more than a year, and he probably has a girlfriend. Or has long moved on from even thinking about me. Or both.

But I don't care. Those eyes, those dimples, that smile, those lips. Rein it in, Pippa.

Dylan snaps his fingers. "Actually, this is perfect that we ran into each other. I was thinking about asking Ben Baxter for some advice on doing a music video, but I don't have his number. The guys and I wrote a new song we're pretty pumped about, and we thought maybe we do a video for it. Ben's doing video stuff at college, right? And his dad runs a big studio?"

Ben Baxter. Half the reason Dylan and I broke up was because he was jealous of Ben. The other half was my jealousy of Muse. Last year, Dylan and Ben couldn't stand to be near each other. Now they're going to make a music video together?

"He should be back in Spalding next week. I'll text you his number."

Dylan gets a funny look on his face and asks, "You still *have* my number, right?"

There's a moment of silence between us, his eyes intent on mine. Me, biting my lip and thinking about how I never replied to his text last year. Finally, I nod.

"Cool. So what about you?" Dylan says.

My heart is pounding again. "Huh?"

"This summer. What're you up to?"

"Oh, um. Me. Right. Spalding. Yeah. I'll be there."

He laughs. "Cool."

Ramona returns and is about to hop back over the counter, but Dylan puts a hand on the counter, to stop her. "You guys are totally done here. Check out the band."

"Thanks again for the rescue, Dylan," Ramona says. "I'm kinda dying to catch them." She nudges my shoulder. "You ready?"

Ready to leave this tiny little space I'm sharing with Dylan McCutter? No thanks. What *I'm* dying to do is throw myself across the counter and invite Dylan to lie on top of me. But that would probably be weird.

But before I can make a fool of myself by opening my mouth, Dylan says, "Go! Go! That's what you came for, not to hang out here." He looks at me. "Maybe I'll see you around."

"Hey, can I get a T-shirt, or what?" some guy behind us barks before I can reply.

"What size?" Dylan says, turning his attention to the small line that's formed again. I hop over the counter, grabbing Ramona's arm to steady myself.

She pulls me close as we head into the venue. "Wow, I did *not* in a million years see that coming."

"Yeah, me either." *Maybe I'll see you around.*

"Remind me again why you let him get away?"

"No clue," I say. But of course, that's not true. She gives me a look and I tell her I'll tell her everything later. She nods and then a second later, we're inside the concert hall, pushing our way through the crowd.

"Hey, there's Matt!" she says, waving wildly. "My boyfriend," she explains to me, and then repeats the line over and over as she pulls me through the crowd. Finally, when we're about three rows from the stage, she stops.

"You have a boyfriend?"

She leans over, her face inches from mine. "No, but it works every time for getting to the front of a crowd." I laugh and then turn my attention to the band. The music's loud and the band is full of energy and within seconds I'm bopping along to the music, singing, swaying.

An hour and a half later we make our way, sweaty and hoarse, out of the venue. We have to walk right by the merch booth and my stomach gets all knotted, but when we reach it, it's already cleared out, the booth dark. No Dylan to be seen.

"You wanna get something to eat?" Ramona says. "I know a great spot a few blocks that way." We walk along 23rd, back towards 5th and into a 24-hour diner, one of those ones with the neon signs, and we slide into a vinyl booth. I text Emmy to let her know what's up.

"All right, spill it," she says once we're seated and the waitress has dropped off plastic-coated menus. I know exactly what she means because I'm still thinking about Dylan too. After I remind her how we broke up, and the text he'd sent, saying that he still thought of me as a friend, she asks the question that I've asked myself a million times.

"Why didn't you just text him back, like, *anything*? Keep the possibility of getting back together alive?"

I fiddle with the metallic corner on the menu. "Did you ever have a friend from camp when you were younger? And you swore to be penpals, and for the first few weeks when you got back home you did write letters and mail them to each other? But then school and sleepovers and other friendships and life got in the way and you kept thinking, I should write, but then you'd forget, and then before you knew it, even though you still wanted to be in touch, you felt weird about it, like too much time had passed and you lost your nerve? Like what if she'd forgotten about you or didn't want to be penpals anymore?"

"Ughhhh. Totally."

"Well, that's what it felt like. Plus, I kept thinking how I was technically the one who broke up with him but he really didn't seem to care. And then he was dating Muse. And then he went away for the summer, and then he went to college and I just felt dumb. Like he's doing all this new cool stuff and why would he want to hear from some ex-girlfriend he'd probably already forgotten about? He'd be like, Who is this, again?"

"Relationships," Ramona says, picking up a menu. "The struggle is real."

I laugh and scan my own menu, realizing that I haven't thought about Tisch in hours. And even though we've been talking about my failed relationship, which is admittedly not the most fun topic, I'm having *fun*. It feels like the first time in forever that I just lived in the moment and haven't been worried about college or my future or my life. Worrying about a guy you used to like is a lot more fun than worrying about an SAT score. But as I look over the menu, not really reading the words, it also hits me that this is what next year could've been like: Ramona and me, ordering food at a diner late on a Friday night, without a curfew and talking and laughing. No worries, at least for a night.

The waitress returns to take our order, pulling a pen and pad from the front pocket of her retro mustard-yellow dress. Ramona looks at me. "You ready?" she says, but she must notice my mood has taken a nosedive.

"We're gonna need some heartbreak shakes," she says to the waitress. "Super sized with sympathy sauce on top."

The waitress stares at Ramona, pen in mid-air. "It's been a long day, ladies. How about two large chocolate milkshakes with whipped cream?"

Over a breakfast of waffles and coffee with David and Emmy in the East Village, I tell them how the meeting with Vishwanathan went. Then I swear them to secrecy: they can't tell Mom. Both disagree—and swear anyway. At the Port Authority I grab a quick selfie of the three of us then hug them goodbye, trying to rein in my thoughts that this might be the last time I see both of them for a long time.

Mom's waiting at the bus depot for me when I arrive home. She hugs me tight. "Maybe we're going to have to do a few more of these one-nighters away to get me used to you being gone," she says, and I don't remind her that I'm supposed to be gone for an entire month in July when I'm backpacking with Dace. I switch gears and tell her about my afternoon with Ramona, including the concert, excluding the sneaking-in part, obvs. But I do tell her about Dylan.

"Wow. How was that?" she asks as she puts my bag in the trunk and we both climb into the car.

"OK, I guess. Just seeing him reminded me how much I liked him, but then also how hurt and mad at him I was. It's hard to have all those feelings about one person."

"Mmm," she says, patting my leg. "Get used to it. That's love." She turns onto Church Street and heads toward home. I stare out the window, thinking about Dylan.

"And the pre-orientation? Did you meet a lot of the instructors?"

"Um, yeah," I say, realizing I didn't really think through what a pre-orientation would involve.

"And what about dorms? Did they talk to you about how that works? Do you get to choose your building?"

My phone dings. It's Ben, announcing his return to Spalding for the summer.

"I'm not sure," I say, distractedly, to Mom as I text Ben back and make a plan to hang out.

"And what about roommates? Is there anyone from Tisch camp you want to be roommates with?"

I look up from my phone. *"Mom,"* I say, with more of an edge than I intend. "So many questions."

She looks over at me. "Pippa, I'm just interested." Then she softens. "It can be a bit overwhelming, huh?"

"I guess."

"Well, don't worry. It's only April. You still have all summer to get ready. Speaking of which, do you think it's still a good idea to travel with Dace? I was thinking it might be better to put off travel till next summer, after you've got a year of college under your belt?"

I look back out the window, watching as the houses zip by. I know what Mom's trying to say. Should I really be going backpacking, spending money instead of making it? Since I didn't get a scholarship? To a school I didn't even get into?

●　●　●

"So let me get this straight," Dace says as we lie on my bed, eating "healthy" root vegetable chips that taste terrible. Dace came over seconds after I got home for our Sleepover Saturdays ritual. I've filled her in on everything. "What you're saying is that this Tisch dude essentially told you to stop being a workaholic and to have fun for the next six weeks?"

"Not exactly," I say, taking a sip of seltzer water.

But Dace pops up off the bed and goes over to my desk, returning with a pen and pad of paper. "SATs, photography, college apps—none of that stuff was my expertise. But fun? *This* I can help you with." She lies down on the bed and puts the pen in her mouth as she thinks. "First up, you can come to Monday Morning Meditation with me."

"That doesn't sound fun."

Dace rolls her eyes. "It's to get you in the zone. Help you focus on having fun. Trust me. Meditation totally helped me switch gears." She starts a list. "You could get your driver's license. Because that opens up a whole new realm of fun."

"You already drive me everywhere I need to go," I say, dismissing thoughts of getting to Hanlan's for garbage picking. "I don't need it."

She writes *Get license* on the list then holds her pen up. "Also! We could go skydiving. I have always wanted to go skydiving. And bungee jumping. Let's save that for our trip—you can jump off the Danube Tower in Austria. That would be cool. Oh, and back-packing around Europe definitely counts."

She writes *Skydive* and *Bungee jump* and *Backpacking around Europe* on the list.

My phone dings with an Instagram notification.

DylMc started following you.

I stare at my phone. Even though post-breakup I unfollowed Dylan first, it still burned when I noticed he'd stopped following me.

Dace gives me a look. "What?"

I show her the screen as I take a sip of bubbly water because NBD or anything.

She squeals.

I can feel my cheeks start to burn. "Do I follow him back? Of course I do. Do I?"

"Wait until tomorrow. Play hard to Instagram."

An hour later, we're lying in my bed, lights out, but all I can think about is Dylan. Is he scrolling through my photos right now? Is he wishing there were photos of me, rather than color-matched flat lays and flowers? I close my eyes, but all I see is Dylan's face, his eyes, that dimple. What is it about being out of sight, out of mind? It's not that I *never* thought about Dylan before seeing him last night, but I had basically exhausted the opportunities to stalk him online—googling him only brings up five results, and nothing new had appeared all year long—so I was forced to make him a memory. But now?

"You still awake?" I ask Dace.

"Hmm?" she murmurs.

"Nevermind."

"You dreaming about McDreamy?"

"Kinda. You think it's been long enough?"

"Def."

I grab my phone and hit the request button on his IG.

"He's probably asleep," I say.

"Mm-hmm."

"I'm not going to look at my phone til morning."

"Mm-hmm."

We continue that dozing off convo for a while, and then my phone dings.

DylMc accepted your friend request.

I want to scour his photos to see every single thing he's posted since we broke up, but at the same time I want to savour it. Maybe I'll only let myself look at one photo a day.

That's it. One picture. Except it's kind of hard to look at only *one* photo. Because obviously his entire gallery loads, and it's only natural that my eyes glance over the whole page. But OK, I'll just put my hand over the photos and click on the first photo. It's a T-shirt that says *Don't stop. Never stop*, which I recognize as a Cherry Blasters line—*our* band. I take it as a sign that I have the go-ahead to look at all his photos.

An hour later I've scrolled through every single

photo in his feed, all the way back to the ones from when we were together. It's all still there. Him and me. Our entire relationship. The bench at the hospital. The gazebo. The picture of us opening our Christmas presents together—our early Christmas in his bedroom. But between then and now? Pictures of him with friends, skiing. On a road trip, playing cards in his dorm room, him at a beach, with a girl. Girl friends, guy friends. His entire year, documented. I click over to my feed and think about what he must have thought, looking at my photos. I'm lame and boring. I barely went to parties, I didn't date, I didn't go on any exciting trips. And even the hard stuff I went through? I didn't document anything on here. It's just an overcurated feed that completely misrepresents my year. If my year were a color, what would it be? Beige. Plain old boring, safe beige.

"Heyyyyyy, Pippaaaaaaaa," Annie drawls, head tilted, approaching me as Dace and I walk the path from the parking lot to the front doors. I look from Annie to Emma, beside her, whose head is also on an angle. I forgot they'd be at school early. Drama club rehearses in the mornings.

"Hey?" I say, raising my eyebrows.

"How are you *doing*?" I know this tone of voice. It's the one everyone—and I mean everyone: the cashier at Duane Reade, the mailman, our neighbors —used on me after Dad died. Why is Annie acting like someone died.

"Fiiiiiiine. How are *you* doing?" I reply, mimicking her tone.

She sighs. "It's just *so* crazy. Like, you of all people?" She shakes her head. "God, you're, like, the benchmark for everyone else. If *you* didn't get into your first choice, with your focus and drive, what's going to happen to the rest of us, amiright?" She looks to Emma beside her and she nods, her black curls springing all over the place.

Um, what?

"Well, I don't know what you'd be worried about, actually. Emma, congratulations on Brown," I say flatly. "And Annie, you're in at UCLA, right? Anyway, I didn't *not* get in."

"But you got *waitlisted*," she says, as though I caught an STI over the weekend. Which I definitely didn't, since I spent Sunday inside, wallowing and watching bad movies with Dace. "What are you going to do?"

"Monday Morning Meditation, for starters," Dace interjects. "That's why we're here at the crack of dawn. We barely slept after that party last night. Come on, Pip. We don't want to be late."

"Um, *what* party was that?" I say to Dace as we head through the front doors.

She throws her head back and laughs. "Give them something else to talk about. Eek, but we really better hurry. Meditation starts in five."

"I didn't think you were serious about me coming to meditation," I say as I open my locker. Usually, while Dace is at Monday Morning Meditation, I edit my photos for photo club. "Not that I'm not appreciative for the convo cut."

Dace turns to me. "You've got something better to do at 8 a.m. that doesn't have anything to do with photography?"

"No, but I don't even have a yoga mat," I say, shoving my backpack in my locker and closing the door.

"I've got you covered." Dace opens her locker and pulls out a mat. "Also, it's called a meditation mat."

●　●　●

There are a dozen girls all sitting on yoga—er, meditation—mats when we enter the gym. For a moment I think about turning right around and fleeing, but Dace loops arms with me and leads me over to a space just big enough for us to both fit our mats. "Unroll and take off your shoes and socks," she whispers.

"Why?"

"It helps you connect with the earth." I don't mention that actually, the pool is in the basement beneath us so we're technically about 20 feet away from the earth.

"Welcome." I look up to see Anisha, a pretty sophomore I've never said two words to, smiling expectantly from a few mats over. "Pippa, right?"

"Right," Dace says. "This is her first Monday Meditation, but I'm sure it's not going to be her last."

"Well, it's nice to have you join us. Find a comfortable position and let us begin." Anisha bows her head and then dings the bell by her knee and places her hands on her bare knees. I sit cross-legged and put my hands on my knees, trying not to squirm.

"Let's close our eyes, and turn our attention inwards," Anisha says in her soothing voice. "Think of your word of intention for today's practice. The one that is going to guide you. It might simply be for this meditation, or it might be the word that gets you through your day. Or even your entire year."

A one-word mantra.

"As you breathe out, exhale your mantra into the meditation space. Engrain the word into your mindfulness experience."

I'm not sure I'm ready for this. We inhale and then as we exhale, the room fills with people's words: *Breathe, Focus, Finish, Calm, Think, Make.* I hear Dace say *Be* beside me.

It's all so earnest and pure that it becomes hard not to be earnest and pure, myself. The word that pops into my head? *Succeed.* Now, more than ever, I need to succeed. That's my word.

Anisha chimes the bell again and then a second later the sounds of seagulls and waves fill the gym from the Bluetooth speaker beside her. I lower my head and stare at the chipped orange polish on my toes. Then close my eyes as Anisha's voice fills the air. "Let's begin this meditation by noticing the posture that you're in. Tune into any sensations in your body that are present to you in this moment. There might be heaviness . . ."

Heaviness? Understatement of the century.

"Pressure . . . Weight . . ."

It's as though this sophomore is inside my brain.

"These sensations may be anywhere in your body, and all you have to do is notice them. Notice what's happening with curiosity and interest. Take a breath. Feel your lungs expanding."

But I can't breathe. My throat feels tight, like it's nothing more than a pinhole. And expanding? All I can think is how I'm supposed to be expanding my skills. Is this really going to count?

"As you breathe, relax. There's nothing you have to do in this moment; be present."

She's totally wrong. There is so much to do. Doing literally nothing won't get me off the waitlist and into Tisch. And will I even prove that I'm doing this without a photo of it? I open my eyes and look around. Everyone's eyes are closed. They look peaceful. Not a care in the world. They've probably all received their acceptance letters and know what they're doing with the rest of their lives. Or, like Anisha, have at least another year before they even have to start thinking about college. Of *course* they're calm. They don't understand the pressure, the weight, the heaviness I feel. Dace has her hands on her knees, palms up. Like a living, breathing skinny blonde Buddha statue.

I can't just sit here.

As slowly and quietly as I can, I shift onto one butt cheek and reach into my jeans pocket and pull out my phone. I make sure it's on silent and then hold it up at chest height and snap a photo of the three girls across from me. The rule of thirds. It would be even better if I could get just a bit closer. I rock onto my knees, off my mat onto the cold gym tile and hold my phone out as far as I can.

Out of the corner of my eye, I see Anisha's eyes flicker open. I freeze, off balance, and tip forward, my phone clattering to the floor. I reach for it, and all three girls in front of me stare at me. I don't have to look around to know everyone is looking at me.

"Are you taking *pictures* during our meditation session?" Anisha's brown eyes narrow to slits.

"I just thought . . . everyone looked so peaceful. It was such an inspiring moment. I wanted to capture it."

"Is this some sort of undercover *Hall Pass* project, Pippa?"

"No." I shake my head. Although an undercover project *would* have probably been a better idea than Monday Morning Meditation or taking a picture of Monday Morning Meditation.

"It's completely disrespectful," Anisha is saying. "I'm going to have to ask you to leave."

For a second I think she's kidding, but then the girl beside her is nodding and glaring at me. "You didn't even ask our permission."

"Were you going to post that picture?"

"Seriously."

Anisha holds up a hand to silence everyone. "Listen, Pippa, it seems like this isn't for you. We get it: you're into photography. But that's not what this is about. Why don't you come back when you're less about documenting the moment and more about being in it?"

All eyes are on me, including Dace, who looks 100 percent mortified. My face burns as I stand up, turn and hurry out of the gym, leaving my mat and Dace behind.

"I don't understand," Lisa says. We're in the photocopy room, a.k.a. *Hall Pass* headquarters. I'm sitting on one of the supply counters that houses photocopy paper, and Lisa's pacing. Everyone else is pretending to mind their own business, but I know they're listening. It's *too* quiet. "I don't understand how you just don't have any Streeters this week? You've been doing Streeters forever. Every Tuesday you submit Streeters. Did you suddenly get amnesia?"

"Kinda," I say.

"Kinda?!"

"Whoa, Lisa, calm down," says Colin, the copy editor, the guy who finds our typos and spelling mistakes. He rubs his shaved head, something he often does while talking. "No one's going to die if we don't find out whether people think we should

71

serve sweet potato fries or regular French fries in the caf."

Lisa glares at him. "Can you go out now and do one, Pippa? We need to fill the space with *something*."

"Well that's not technically true," I say. We used to be a paper, but now everything's online, so it's not as if there'd be this blank space, anywhere. Just a page we don't update. No one's *really* going to notice. Or care, for that matter.

"She's right," Colin chimes in.

"We have standards," Lisa says. "Expectations to meet. People rely on us. We're an important part of this school and we can't just not do regular columns simply because one of us forgot. We'll just post late. Go out now and get something. Anything."

"I left my camera at home." I bite my lip.

"You *what*?" Lisa's voice goes up an octave. "Use your phone."

"I . . . I think I need to take a break from *Hall Pass*."

"A break?" Lisa's voice goes into an even higher register. "Six weeks before the end of the school year? That's how you want to go down in Spalding High history? As a quitter?"

"I'm not quitting . . ." I say, but of course that's exactly what I'm doing.

"I can take over," Devyn says. Devyn's a sophomore who writes the horoscopes as well as a weekly column about being adopted by two lesbians. She also often takes pictures at the basketball games because her boyfriend's on the team.

"Great," Lisa says. "Devyn, you're on Streeters

till the end of the year. Colin, take Pippa off the masthead. That's what you want, right, Pippa?"

Is that what I want? I don't say anything for a second, hoping that Lisa will tell me that I'm obviously having a tough day. That they can't lose me as a photographer. But she just stares at me. I look around at everyone else in the room. All eyes are on me. "Yeah, that's what I want."

And just like that, I'm no longer a photographer at *Hall Pass*.

I hope Vishwanathan is happy.

●　●　●

I walk home, wondering what I'm going to do with my free time. *Hall Pass* meetings have been every Tuesday all year long. Mom always works the late shift on Tuesdays and leaves me something frozen to heat up for dinner. But with leaving school early, there's a chance I'll see her before she leaves for work. And I'm going to have to explain why I'm not in *Hall Pass* anymore.

A golf cart zips toward me on the sidewalk, the driver beeping the horn like crazy.

I step off the sidewalk but the cart screeches to a halt beside me. The guy behind the wheel takes off his New York Yankees ball cap and grins.

"Ben! You are such a freak." I smile. I haven't seen Ben since spring break when he was home for a few days.

"Freaking *awesome* you mean. I thought I was picking you up at school in, like, an hour?"

"I totally forgot."

Seconds later I'm sitting in his passenger seat. Ben is looking good. He's been home from the University of Utah a few times—the usual holidays—but I'm still caught off guard every time. Blond hair, blue eyes, golden tan even though it's only May. It's really such a shame there is absolutely no physical attraction there.

"What happened to hanging on the weekend?" Ben says as he hits the gas and we take off down the sidewalk.

"Sorry. Long story—I got waitlisted for Tisch, went to New York and spent the rest of the weekend wallowing."

"Whoa."

"Yeah."

"So what are you going to do?"

"Oh you know, stop taking photos, and find other fascinating hobbies to fill my time and enrich my life to show how well-rounded I am in the hopes that they reconsider."

"At least you're not bitter." Ben gives me a long look, but I look straight ahead, then scream as a white ball of fluff crosses in front of the golf cart. I clutch on to the roof as Ben swerves, rumbling over a neatly manicured front lawn, but narrowly misses the dog. A woman glares at us, then scoops up the dog.

"Close one," he says, once we're back on the sidewalk again.

"Now can we talk about why you're driving a golf cart? Beemer in the shop?"

"You're looking at the hottest summer employee at White Water World."

"Ben Baxter has a summer job at the water park? What happened to working with your dad?" When Ben and I last talked summer plans, he told me he was going to be working in one of his dad's production company's satellite offices just outside Buffalo for the summer.

"Turns out he 'forgot' he was going to be in San Fran all summer. But Oksana was going to be in the office so I could see her every day," he says sarcastically.

"Ouch." Ben and his dad have had a hot and cold relationship that seemed to be in the lukewarm temp—his dad came to visit him in Park City in the winter, and they had a great bonding weekend snowboarding. But then a few months ago his dad got the clichéd twentysomething girlfriend who Ben doesn't like. Still, Ben's taking video production in college, following in his dad's footsteps, like I want to follow in my dad's.

"Whatever. How bad can it be, relaxing in the sun, right?"

"I guess," I say, still thinking how he's not exactly following his dream. "It's probably not too late to find something film-related. The park can't be opening for at least another month, can it?"

"Today was my first day. It's just maintenance stuff for now, until the end of June." He slows as he approaches an intersection, and waits for a bunch of cars to pass. "It's only one summer. I've got years till it really matters. What about you? What's your plan again?"

"Dace and I are supposed to be backpacking in July, but . . . I should probably get a job actually. Only I'm dreading telling Dace because she'll be so mad at me. I don't know what I'm going to do."

"Well, I can hook you up, you know, serving cotton candy or something." He winks.

"I still don't get the golf cart."

"They use these golf carts to get around the park and I thought, why not just take one home?"

"How many times have I told you not to listen to the little voice in your head with the terrible ideas?"

"I'm sorry, didn't you just tell me that you're supposed to be doing wild and crazy things? You could learn a thing or two from me. Borrow a golf cart, drive it around town. It's actually really fun." Ben slams on the brakes and hops out, then points to the seat. "All yours. It's like riding a bike. Only without the wedgie." He comes around to my side.

"For the record," I say as I scooch over to his side, "I didn't say wild and crazy and I'm not sure why everyone seems to interpret doing non-photography stuff as wild and crazy." I look at the controls in front of me—way simpler than a car.

"Now you hit the gas. Except. I think this thing is electric. So you press the pedal or whatever."

"Or whatever? Not helpful." I press my foot down lightly on the gas pedal and we lurch forward. I slam on the brake and we skid to a stop. Finally I get the feel for the pedals and soon we're zooming forward.

"See?" Ben asks. "Easy. You can barely tell you don't have your license yet."

"It's on the to-do list."

Ben points down the street to Scoops. "Pit stop for ice cream?"

I shrug. "Sure." There was a time when I couldn't come to Scoops, because of what happened here, with Dad. Each time I caught a glimpse of the ice cream place where I used to spend hours working, I would think about that day he died. It was both the best afternoon and the worst all rolled into one. As though having this perfect date with my dad had to be followed up with the worst moment of my life—seeing him in pain, having to take him to the hospital. The beginning of the end of his life. I guess time does heal, because it feels like so long ago. Like I was a different person. In therapy, Dr. Judy told me that when I feel a panic attack coming on, I have to block out the past and focus only on the moment. To remove the association of what's causing me to panic. I'm pretty good at that now, but it means that I block out all of the past a lot of the time—the bad times, when Dad was sick, but also the good times, when it was Dad and Mom and me. The three of us. I barely think about the vacations we took, or games we used to play on Friday nights together, because even thinking about happy stuff makes me sad. I can't remember Dad's voice anymore, or the funny turns of phrase he would use. I can't remember which side he parted his hair on, or what his hands looked like. It's all fading away.

"Pippa?" I turn to see Ben standing beside the golf cart, hands on the roof, leaning over to look at me. "You OK?"

I nod, blinking back tears, and get out of the cart.

Bells chime as Ben pushes open the door to Scoops and holds it for me. The place is empty except for a girl behind the counter. "Hey guys," she says, and I recognize her: Callie.

Back when I volunteered at the hospital, Callie worked at the cafeteria. I thought there was something going on between her and Dylan, but it turned out they were just childhood friends. I think about this now, and how my relationship with Dylan seemed to be continuously fraught with my jealousy and misunderstandings. Callie, then Ben and Muse . . .

"You're not working at the hospital anymore?" I say, walking up to the counter.

She sighs. "I needed a change. This is pretty good except for the fact that my hand is always so cold."

"I remember that feeling," I say. "I used to work here. Oh, hey, this is Ben. Ben, Callie."

Callie gives a quick smile to Ben, then turns back to me. "You worked here? Maybe you can help me. All my waffle cones have holes in the bottom and everyone's complaining that the ice cream drips out."

I nod. "You just have to roll them tighter than you think."

"Who knew serving ice cream could be such a challenge." She rolls her eyes.

"And on that note, I think I'll have mine in a cup," Ben says. "Chocolate chip. You?"

"Tiger tail. Cup too." I smile.

The bells chime and I turn to see my old boss, Rita, come through the front door. She glances our way but either doesn't recognize me or can't be bothered to acknowledge me, walking straight into the back through the Employees Only door. She was my least favorite part about working at Scoops. Seriously, how can you be grumpy when you own a shop that makes customers so happy?

Callie must feel the same way because she seems to tense up as she scoops our ice cream, handing it to us then moving over to the cash. "Would you like six muffins with that?" Callie asks as she punches the buttons on the cash register.

"Did you just ask us if we wanted muffins with our ice cream?" Ben laughs.

"Yes, I did," Callie says, smiling broadly, and her voice is overly cheerful, sort of like she's on an infomercial. "They're freshly baked today. Blueberry or carrot. Perfect for the morning so you don't have to think about what to have for breakfast!" She's not blinking, but she's still smiling. Then she leans over the counter and talks super quietly, without moving her lips. "Shut up and don't make fun of me. My boss is watching and I'm not upselling the muffins enough. Please buy some muffins?"

"What? No one wants muffins. It's an ice cream shop. People want ice cream!" Ben slams his hand on the counter, laughing.

"I'd love six muffins. Blueberry. Please," I say extra loudly. Callie exhales and smiles at me. "Thanks."

I hand her a twenty.

I pull Ben away from the counter and we move to a booth. "That was mean."

"*That* was ridiculous."

"I feel bad for her. I'm glad I didn't have to do that when I worked here." I think about Callie, working at the ice cream shop now, two years after graduating from high school. Is this what's going to happen to me if I don't get into Tisch? Am I going to be back working at the same place I worked when I was a sophomore, making minimum wage for the rest of my life and serving my friends when they're home from college for the summer?

"I bet she wishes she went to college," I say aloud.

"Not everyone wants to go to college," Ben says, sliding in beside me. He selfies us and taps the screen a few times. A few seconds later, my phone vibrates. "Take the tag off me," I say. "I don't do selfies."

He gives me a look. "Lighten up."

"What? I like to keep my online persona professional."

"You mean boring. I noticed. How many likes do your pics get?"

I roll my eyes. "Not everyone cares about likes. I care about having curated work." I think of my color theme, how since the meeting with Vishwanathan I haven't posted a single photo. Not even the great golden hour pics that I'd planned to post this week.

"My stuff's curated too. I post hot selfies, shirtless selfies and drunken selfies. See?"

"Ben, I've seen your Instagram."

"The difference between our feeds? Mine looks like it's me. Yours doesn't look like you. Yours looks like a museum. Bunch of boring shots of stuff. It wouldn't kill you not to take everything so seriously."

"I don't. Just photography."

"Yeah, and all you do is photography."

I grab my phone, stick out my tongue, take a selfie and then show it to Ben. "See? I can be *so* crazy."

"You going to post it?"

"Of course not."

"Post it and we'll talk."

After school is photo club and I'm dreading telling the group that I'm resigning as president. Obviously I don't want to admit that I've been waitlisted to people who haven't heard, but I don't want to lie about Tisch any more than I already have, so I fumble my way through an announcement then shift gears. "Since Brooke is going to be president next year, I think it makes sense for her to get a jump-start, so that if there are changes she wants to make, you can think about them over the summer. Then really dive into things in the fall."

Everyone looks mildly bored by my announcement, which is really not the reaction I was hoping for. I wasn't expecting tears or groveling, but an objection or two would've been nice. Instead, everyone focuses on Brooke, who looks thrilled. "This is great. I do have a lot of ideas, actually," she says and grabs her phone. "I've made a document—it's kind of rough because I planned to work on it through the summer—but let's jump in anyway. There are some changes I wanted to make. First, we've been doing the same format forever . . ." Everyone is totally engrossed in what she's saying. I stand up, grab my bag and head out the door.

I'm halfway past the parking lot when I hear my name. I turn to see Hank waving at me from his car, a beat-up old Ford Focus that's mostly gold except for the driver's door, which is, for some reason, green. He's had the car forever and spends a lot of his free time tinkering with it, but it never seems to look any different. Also, he's part of a Corvette Club, but he doesn't actually drive a Corvette. He's a real man of mystery when it comes to automobiles. "Want a ride?" he calls.

"Sure, thanks." I head over.

"Want to drive?" That's the thing about Hank—he's always offering to let me drive his car, even though Mom never lets me. She says it's because I haven't been taking my lessons.

"Are you sure? I haven't been practicing." Back when Dad was alive, I used to take driving lessons every week, and Dad would let me practice any time we had to go out. But I stopped taking lessons after he died and I started getting panic attacks. And then this year, when I had to retake my SATs, driving lessons felt like one extra thing I shouldn't be spending time or money on.

He tilts his head and smiles. "Have you seen this thing?" He waves a hand over the hood. "What's the worst that could happen?" I take the keys and I open the driver's side door and slide in. Hank gets in on the passenger side.

I adjust the mirrors, turn the key in the ignition then slowly back out of the parking space. "My instructor had a Ford Focus, so if there's any chance of me *not* crashing a car, this would be it."

"Good to know." Neither of us speaks for a bit, the only sound the talk radio chatter. "Aren't you usually at Photo Club on Wednesdays?" Hank asks once I'm cruising along Elm Street.

"Only a few of us could make it today so we decided to cancel," I say, kind of surprised how easily the lie comes out.

As the talk radio hosts blather on, my thoughts go to Dad. How he loved listening to podcasts any time he was in the car—didn't matter if it was a road trip or a five-minute ride to pick up a pizza at Pete's. When I was driving, though, I was allowed to put on the music of my choice. I would purposely take the long route to wherever we were going, just to torture him with whatever song I was obsessed with at the moment. Well, that and the fact I usually avoided left turns. Fact: it doesn't actually take any longer to get somewhere if you're only turning right.

"You're a good driver," Hank says. "Maybe it's not my business, but is there a reason you're not taking your test?"

I grip the steering wheel, deciding how much to share. "Avoidance, mostly. I guess the SAT fiasco was as big a failure as I could handle."

"I don't think that your SAT retake counts as a

failure. Think about how much time you spent visiting Dace, being a good friend to her, and worrying about her when you weren't out visiting her. You shouldn't beat yourself up about it."

"Yeah." I pull onto my street. "Can I ask you something now?"

"Shoot."

"Do all the teachers talk?"

"It definitely helps, since not many of us know sign language." He chuckles. "Sorry, I'll be serious. What do you mean?"

"Nothing. Or, I just meant, like, about stuff. Like if one teacher knows something, do you all know? Like, say, if someone gets detention or cheats on a test or something. Is that what you guys spend your time talking about in the lounge?"

I pull into the driveway and put the car in park.

"Hmmm," he says. "Well, there's a lot of talk about sports. Baseball, football, a bit of golf, that sort of thing. But if you're asking if I heard about you getting waitlisted, yes, it came up. I don't know that all the teachers know, but Mr. Aquila asked me how things were going for you at home, and it came out."

"Great. When did you find out?"

"Yesterday."

"Did you tell my mom?"

"No."

"Are you going to?"

"No."

"Positive?"

I undo my seatbelt and turn to face Hank. He's already looking at me. "Pippa, whatever your reason is for telling your mom you got in when you didn't is your business. I don't agree with it and I think you've got to decide when you're going to tell her the truth, but this is between you two."

"I've got it under control. So you don't have to worry."

"All right. Hey—" Hank reaches over and puts a hand on my shoulder. "You know yourself best. And if you ever want to talk about anything, in confidence, just let me know."

"OK. Thanks." We get out of the car and I hand Hank the keys. He moves to the driver's side. "You're not coming in?"

He shakes his head. "Got to grab Charley from school."

"Oh, right," I say, realizing that it was probably out of his way to drive home with me. "Thanks for the ride."

"Anytime, Pippa. I mean it."

Once I'm in my bedroom, I log on to the DMV road test site and click the first available appointment. Here goes nothing.

Mom's sitting at the kitchen table drinking coffee and reading, and she doesn't look up when I come into the kitchen.

"Morning," I say.

She looks a little startled and flips the papers over. "You're up early."

I yawn. "Garbage picking day."

"You want me to make you something to eat before you go?"

"Nah," I say. "I'll just bring a muffin." I grab one of the guilt muffins I bought at Scoops.

"Let me grab you the good traveler." She shuffles down the hall in her slippers. "I left it in the car."

When I hear the front door open, I flip over the papers she was looking at. *Application for Mortgage.*

Mortgage? Why would we need a mortgage? When my grandparents moved into a retirement home, they gave their house to my mom and dad. So why would Mom need one now?

Mom returns with the blue metal travel mug that doesn't leak even if you knock it over, washes it, then fills it with coffee and hands it to me. It's only then that I register she's wearing her scrubs.

"You're working again this morning?" I ask. Normally, if she works a night shift, she has the next day off.

She takes a sip of her coffee and nods. "Can't keep me away. Good news is I'm leaving in ten minutes. So I can give you a ride to Hanlan's if you want?"

"Please."

I open my mouth several times to bring up the mortgage papers, but it feels like one secret will lead to another and I'm not ready to have an all-out honesty session with Mom. Maybe one day, but not yet. So instead, I turn the volume up on the radio, and stare out the window as Mom drives.

●　●　●

I'm climbing the hill to the entrance of the park when it's like someone has sneak-attack ice bucket challenged me. It's a full on downpour and in seconds my hair is sopping wet and stuck to my face. I race toward the shed for cover, panicked for my camera, then remember I don't have it. For once in my life, I'm glad. My phone in the front pocket of my pants is somehow dry, covered by my long sweater. My school bag is soaked as I shrug it off my back and leave it on the floor of the shed and start grabbing my supplies. I pause, then grab a second garbage bag, rip a hole in it and pull it over my head to cover my clothes. I grab a third and tie it under my chin to create a hood. Then I head out into the field and start picking up garbage. I walk the field in straight lines, up and down, up and down, and start to get into a groove. When I reach the concessions side of the field, I stand under the awning for a minute and watch the rain coming down. The thunking of rain on the tin roof above me is hypnotizing. I pull out my phone to check the time, and then flip over to my camera and take a photo of the waterfall streaming off the roof. Then I flip the camera to look at myself. I look ridiculous.

I snap a selfie and post it to Instagram. A minute later, there's already a comment, thanks to Dace.

Hey Kylo Ren, where's your lightsaber?
#starwarsday #maythefourth

I check the date—she's right. It's the fourth of May. I laugh and tuck my phone in my jeans. The rain makes me work quickly and 20 minutes later I'm putting my filled garbage bag back into the shed. I make my way down the hill to the sidewalk, and that's when I see him. Standing in the rain, holding an umbrella, wearing a blue raincoat, worn jeans and high-top Vans. Dylan. My heart feels like it decided to take a leap up my chest to sit directly in my throat, preventing me from breathing, swallowing, anything. I press my lips together to stop myself from all-out grinning at him, because I am so happy to see him and not only because it's pouring and he's holding an umbrella.

"Need a ride?" he calls, giving me a half-smile, revealing that dimple. I feel my face flush. But seriously? How would he even know that I'm here?

"Really?" I say and he looks at me for a split second, then runs his hand over his chin, and looks around. He shakes his head. "Oh, no, sorry, I wasn't *offering* a ride . . ." My face flushes and I feel mortified. "I was just asking if you *needed* a ride. You know, just curious." He grins. "Nice look, by the way." And I remember that I'm still wearing my black garb. But he moves closer, holding out his umbrella, and I step under it. My face is inches from his chest, so close that I can smell his oh-so-Dylan smell. It's just soap, but it must be the *same* soap he used to use when we were together.

Focus, Pippa. Breathe. But that only makes me inhale his good Dylan smell even more. "How'd you know I was here?"

"You're kidding, right? Who *doesn't* know you're here? Have you seen your post?"

I pull the garbage bag off my head and pull out my phone. The screen is filled with alerts, and when I open my Instagram, I see I have more than a hundred likes and a dozen comments.

I try not to act like it's a big deal but I've never had more than a handful of likes on any photo.

"So what exactly are you doing here?" he asks, leading me over to his car.

"Community service."

"Ahh. Murder or armed robbery?" He opens the passenger door for me. "Yes, my dad still has this car." I slide onto the blue vinyl, and it's as though I'm entering a time warp, instantly transported back in time to my junior year, my first real date with Dylan when we came, in this car, to Hanlan's Field to see the Cherry Blasters.

Dylan slides into the driver's seat, puts the wet umbrella in the back then starts the car.

"So seriously, community service?" he says as we pull out of the parking lot.

"For school. You know, to graduate."

"Ahh. I'm surprised you didn't clock enough hours at the hospital. You were certainly there a lot." His tone is teasing and my stomach flip-flops.

"I kind of thought the same thing, actually." I clear my throat. Be cool, Pippa. "But I have a handful more hours to do. So, um, what's it like being back home?"

He exhales. "Weird. Like being a kid again, kind of? Truthfully, it's kind of the reason I didn't want to come back. Living with my parents again, with my mom calling me from work to make sure I get out of bed. Speaking of which, I should text her to tell her I'm up, driving around, going for breakfast with you . . ."

"We're going for breakfast?"

"Was that only in my head? Surely picking up all those hotdog wrappers made you ravenous?"

I laugh. "Obviously."

"Anyway, what was I saying?"

"Being home. Weird. Your mom." I think back

to the fight we had last year, how I thought he was being lazy because he was sleeping in while I was at school. Did I feel like a nag, just like his mom?

"Oh yeah. It feels a bit like my mom forgets I'm home for summer vacation—like she's paranoid I'm going to regress to last year. Admittedly it was a waste of a gap year, but that feels like an entire lifetime ago."

I think about how if Dylan hadn't stayed home last year, we wouldn't have been together. I wonder if he thinks we were a waste of time too.

"Anyway, I was worried about that. Regressing. But there are reasons I'm glad to be back." He looks over at me, and we lock eyes for a moment. Dylan turns down a side street, a street I recognize as the way to the Orange Turtle, a diner we used to go to when we were together.

"One of those reasons is my dad—he had a heart attack in February."

"Oh no. Is he OK?"

"He's recovering. They caught it in time. He woke up with chest pains at, like, four in the morning. They say that's often when it happens. When you're coming out of REM, your heart rate speeds up because of the adrenaline. He woke my mom up and told her he thought they should go to the hospital. She was all panicked, obviously, and was asking him if she should call 911, but he was like, No, no, you just drive me. So they're in the car and driving to the hospital and my mom stops at a red light—there's no one around—and he was like, 'Neema, I don't think you should stop at any lights.' My poor mom. Can you imagine?"

My thoughts go straight to my drive with my dad. When he had such severe pain—not a heart attack but the tumor that killed him—and I had to drive him to the hospital.

"That's awful. I'm sorry."

"Yeah." He looks at me. "Actually, when my mom was telling me about it, it was weird. I thought of you. With your dad."

"With my dad, it turned out it actually wouldn't have mattered how quickly I drove. With your mom, that's a lot of pressure."

"Yeah. She blames herself for not getting him to the hospital fast enough. He had some damage to his arteries. They had to do a triple bypass. It wasn't even like he was out of shape. He golfs, plays squash, runs . . ."

"Is he going to be OK?"

Dylan nods. "Yeah. The recovery is long. Like a year to even get back to where he was. Anyway, that made it better, coming home. A purpose, you know? Plus the band and the Hanlan's gig and . . ." He gives me that dimple.

"I'm glad you're back. You know, because of the free ride to school. And breakfast."

"Who said the breakfast was free? You know I'm Dutch by birth, right?"

"You are not."

"I am one-eighth Dutch. I'm practically a von Trapp."

"The von Trapps were Austrian."

He pulls into the Orange Turtle parking lot. "That's another of the eighths. I'm at least 10 percent positive." He turns off the ignition. "I haven't been here in forever."

"Yeah, me either."

The rain has let up a little but I still hurry inside, the scent of sugary French toast and coffee hitting me, and I breathe it in and try to calm myself down. I'm here. With Dylan. "I'm going to wash my hands. You know, garbage picking and all," I say, heading to the back of the diner. When I return, Dylan's in a booth. We used to always sit at the counter, but I don't let myself overanalyze whether there's meaning behind him choosing to sit across from me rather than side by side.

The mix of natural sunlight and the glow from the faux-votives on each table makes the lighting perfect. I think of all the times I've taken pictures in here. Back before I limited myself to color schemes. I slide onto the vinyl seat and pick up my menu. After we order, we talk about music and movies and Boston and Dace and it all feels so easy. Like nothing weird ever happened between us, and I wonder if it's just me that feels this way.

The bells on the door jangle, and I look over to see Ben walk in. For a second I get a flashback to last year and our weird love triangle. But then I remind myself that things have changed. Ben and I are friends. Dylan and I are . . . I don't know what we are. I wave to Ben and he saunters over.

"Well, isn't this some sort of weird reverse déjà

vu," he says, grinning. "McCutter." Dylan stands and slaps hands with Ben like they're old pals.

"Hey Ben. How you doing?"

Ben nods. "Good, dude. Hey, I was going to call you today to go over everything for the video. My guy has a couple of questions for you and some ideas to run by you, and then we just have to lock down the timing and location and stuff like that."

"Cool. I'm excited," Dylan says, sitting back down. "You wanna join us?"

Ben shoves his hands in his pockets. "Nah. I'm just gonna grab a coffee to go. See you guys later." He turns back. "Oh by the way, nice selfie, Greene."

Once Ben's out of earshot I turn back to Dylan. "*That* would never have happened last year."

"Yeah, you're probably right," Dylan says. "That seems like forever ago, huh?"

I nod. "So the video—you're really doing it."

"Yeah. You should hear the song. It's called 'Remember When.' I wrote it in the winter. I think . . . I think you'd like it."

The waitress puts our plates in front of us. Dylan stares down at his plate. Two eggs, two sausages and toast and fruit, but it's sort of glommed together in the center of the plate.

"Wow, has the food here always looked this terrible or have I just forgotten?"

"Always. But it tastes so good." I want to say *Like our theory.* Back when Dylan and I were getting together, we had a theory: food that looks good tastes bad. And vice versa. We would text each other pictures of terrible-looking food.

I want to remind him, but before I can decide if it's too weird, he says, "Like our food alerts."

"You remember those?" I stab a slice of bacon with my fork.

He raises his eyebrows. "It was just last year. I'm not *that* old." He rearranges the food and then turns his plate to me. He's made a face. "Meet Bob." He jabs his fork into his eggs and makes a squealing sound. "My eye, my eye."

I laugh.

"You still take pics of that kind of stuff?" he asks.

I shake my head. "Not really."

"I kinda noticed on your Insta. It's pretty . . . professional."

"Yeah. You can call it boring; Ben did."

"Except today. That was a funny post, friend." He pulls out his phone. "You've got a lot of likes." Twenty likes, for me, is *a lot*.

But all I can think about is the word "*friend.*"

"I can't believe I posted that. I never post selfies and then the one I do? Scary."

He shrugs. "It's real. And funny. And people love Star Wars."

"So much for my curated feed."

He gives me a look. "Is that what you were doing before?"

"Yeah. You know, so people know that I'm a photographer. And in case the Tisch people were looking. I have to care what they think of me."

"Since when? You always do your own thing, you're confident in what you do and it works out like it's all supposed to work out. Like it did. You got into Tisch. Though I have to say, I can't imagine you got in because of your Instagram." He takes a bite of his toast.

"What do you mean?"

He shrugs. "Flowers? Stuff arranged just so on a white table? It's very . . . safe."

I don't say anything. Is he right? Is my Instagram— something I worked so hard to make perfect—what actually influenced Tisch not to admit me?

"Hey."

I look up.

"Why the long face?"

"I didn't get into Tisch."

Dylan lets out a low whistle. "That sucks."

"Yeah. That's why I was in New York. I got wait-listed. And I didn't apply anywhere else. So now I'm trying to switch things up. Do things differently." I take a bite of toast, but it's dry in my mouth. I can feel tears welling up.

"Hey." He touches my arm. "You should just be yourself. That post today? It was funny. And ridiculous. Like you. That was the Pippa I knew and—" He takes his hand off my arm and picks up his coffee to take a sip. "Anyway, I think that's the kind of stuff that'll make Tisch love you."

"Maybe," I say, though I'm not convinced. And totally overwhelmed. I check the time on my phone. "Shoot, I should go."

We get up and walk to the cash. Dylan pulls out his wallet. "You're in luck. I'm not actually feeling very Dutch today. Besides, I feel bad for you— picking garbage."

"So you're taking pity on your ex-girlfriend?"

"Ex has such a negative connotation. We're friends, right, buddy?" He knocks shoulders with me, then hands his bank card over to the cashier.

Buddies. Friends. Is that what we are? Is that what we're destined to be?

● ● ●

"I can't figure out if I *want* to wear something sexy or if I think that I *should* be wearing something sexy," Dace says as we sift through the racks of pyjamas at Target. "Like, do I want to look good, or do I want to be comfy? How do I want to be remembered?"

"Good question," I say, running a flannel unicorn onesie between my fingers.

"Or pointless? Like, who we are here, at Spalding High, won't even matter in two months. No one I meet in Europe is going to know if I was popular or a loser, if I ran every club or skipped school. If I had to go away to get help . . ."

"That's a good thing."

"Yeah. It *is* a good thing. But it made me realize that I seem to really *care* what people think about me."

"No you don't. At all. That's what's *so* great about you."

Dace gives me a look. "Excuse me? I care so much what people think. Not like you. You never care."

"What are you talking about? Dylan said the same thing but all I care is what people think. My whole year has been about trying to be the perfect Tisch candidate. And sucking at it."

She throws an arm around my shoulder. "We're a couple of wannabes."

"My point is—oh, what is my point? Dace, I don't have any identity without photography. You saw that at meditation. Even Anisha was like, You're the photography chick. And then because it was uncomfortable to try to do anything without a camera, I ruined that. I don't know who I am without a camera. And I'm always thinking, you would have no problem changing who you are, or what you do. You're always reinventing yourself. Your look, your attitude."

Dace shows me the screen of her phone. "JFTR, you have 204 followers since that Star Wars pic. And don't you see, Pippa? You know who you are. What you love. Me? I can't figure it out. Oh, I think I'm going to be a model but I can't be one so now I'm just trying out everything, trying to figure it out."

My phone dings. I look at the screen.

"What's wrong?" Dace says.

"Ben just asked us if we want to be extras in the music video. Dylan's music video. They're shooting it at White Water World tomorrow morning."

Dace's jaw drops dramatically. "Yes! This calls for a stop in the swimsuit department."

A second later my phone dings again. Dylan. Must be about the video. But it's not. Two eggs, two sausages. That's what's on my screen. He's texting me pictures of his breakfast?

Dylan: File our breakfast under Places Named for Things They Have Nothing to Do With. Orange Turtle. No such thing as an orange turtle. Not a single orange turtle in this joint.

"Helloooo," Dace says sticking her hand between my face and my screen.

I show her the screen. "Is this weird he's not mentioning the video?"

"Call him on it," Dace says simply.

My fingers won't type. But what do I say?

"No." Dace shakes her head. "Actually *call* him."

A second later, he answers.

"Ben asked Dace and me to be in your video."

"Excellent. You're cool with skipping school?"

Crap. School. "I was wondering why didn't *you* ask me to be in your video?"

"He's making all the calls. But I thought that makes it no pressure for you. So that if you said yes, then *I* could ask you what I was really hoping you'd do. Your part in the video."

"What do you mean?"

"There's this scene, and in it, I need to kiss a girl."

"You need to?"

"Well, I want to. For the video. It's, like, the story of the song."

"OK."

"And I want . . . well, I was hoping, that girl could be you."

My palms feel sweaty and I grip the phone tighter. "So we're going to kiss."

"If you say yes."

I take a deep breath. Turning down the opportunity to kiss Dylan again, even if it's just for a video? Not an option. "One condition. Being 'the girl' in a video? It's not really my thing. I'm the girl behind the camera. You know? So I'll do it, I'll be in the scene, but I want to shoot the video. Stills. A behind the scenes look at the video, to document it all."

"That'd be awesome. Of course. Whatever you want. Thank you."

"OK. Um, OK. See you tomorrow."

I hang up, shove my phone in my pocket and lean against the racks of clothes. What did I just agree to?

"Finally," Dace says, her arms laden with Lycra suits. "Everything cool?"

I nod. "So we're skipping school, huh?" I exhale. "This is a new one for me."

"Now we just have to get you to wear a swimsuit that's not black."

I groan dramatically (all part of the plan) as Mom and I are eating cereal at the kitchen table the next morning. "I forgot to tell you that the dentist booked me for a cleaning at 10 a.m. this morning," I say between spoonfuls of Cheerios.

"Really? Shoot. I'm working at 9, so I can't drive you."

"They charge if you don't give 24 hours' notice to cancel," I say, then add, "at least, that's what the message said."

"Anything important in class this morning?"

"No," I say, shaking my head.

"You OK to take the bus there and back?"

"Sure. I can read. I don't mind."

"Well, all right. Remind them while you're there to book your next appointment for when you're home from college on Christmas break."

My stomach clenches. "OK. Can you call the school to let them know?"

"Sure. I'll call when I get in to work."

Upstairs, I shove my new bathing suit in my bag, along with a small towel, then take a minute to apply my makeup. It's been a while since I wore any. The waterproof mascara does give me longer, thicker lashes. With the new lipgloss Dace gave me I sort of look like a girl who belongs in a music video.

Now to get out of the house without Mom seeing—not because I'm not allowed to wear makeup, but because she'll know something's up if she notices. Mom's in her room. "Bye!" I shout and dash through the front door. Ten minutes later, Dace pulls up beside me, as planned, while I'm walking along Elm. She grins as I climb in the car, then whistles.

"Mascara?" she says.

"It's no big deal."

"I hope it's waterproof," she says.

The water park isn't technically in Spalding. It's in this stretch of no-man's land between Spalding and the next town over. Years and years ago, the water park used to be part of a hotel, but the owners let the hotel get so rundown that they had to shut it down, but no one ever demolished it, so it's just this desolate, decrepit-looking building, with lots of dusty windows. Past the hotel are the gates to the water park, where a security guard stands with a clipboard.

"Closed for a private function," he says.

Dace nods. "We're here for the video."

She points to our names on his list, he checks us

off, then opens the gate. "Head to the wave pool," he says.

The empty amusement park hardly looks like the setting for a music video. The concession stands are empty, the games boarded up. And without anyone around, the place looks desolate. There's a five-minutes-after-the-apocalypse vibe to the place. Past the information booth we follow an arrow to the wave pool. And there's Ben, with a megaphone, and a bunch of people milling about.

"OK, so all the extras are there, obviously," Ben says, pointing to a group of girls and guys a little older than us, all wearing their bathing suits, some of them with hoodies, others wrapped in towels.

Dace moves toward the group and I follow her, but Ben grabs my arm. "Not you. I hear you've got a bigger role in this thing," he teases.

I hold up my camera. "I'm shooting it." But my face is hot.

"Uh huh. Just head over there, OK?" Ben points to the band, who are setting up their gear in front of the lifeguard station, at the head of the wave pool, under the sign that says DEEP END. I spot Dylan just as he looks up, meeting my eye. He raises an arm and smiles, then walks toward me.

"You ready?" He says. Am I ready? It's not so much that people will see this video, even though I suppose it will live on YouTube forever, or as long as YouTube's around, but it's that I'll know that I was in a video. It's just not who I am. Am I making too big a deal about something that's just supposed to be fun? I nod cautiously, and Dylan continues.

"So one thing I didn't mention on the phone: you know the reason I want you to be in the video is because you're the kind of girl who would *never* be in a video, right?"

"You know just what to say."

Ben whistles way too loudly on the bullhorn and begins instructing us on what to do and where to go. He's got a handheld camera in one hand, the bullhorn in the other. There's another guy he points out named Jake, who's got a waterproof camera and is going to shoot from underneath the water. Everyone's moving into position and since I'm not in the video until the last 20 seconds of the song, I grab my camera and begin moving around the pool, snapping from various angles. The band goes through the first half of the song a few times, and as I'm shooting, the lyrics start to sink in. About a guy and a girl and the relationship they used to have. Then Ben calls to me. "Pippa, we need you now."

I walk over to my stuff and tuck my camera under my towel, then take off my T-shirt and shorts, revealing my polka dot bathing suit. Dace catches my eye and gives me an encouraging nod. I know that maybe no one will ever really see this video, but I also know it's important to Dylan and the band and Ben and even everyone else who's here, in on this project.

I can do this. I climb into the water with everyone else, and Ben explains that he'll give me the cue to go under. "Jake will be under the water, but just ignore him. You won't have a lot of time, obviously, because you have to hold your breath." Then he turns to Dylan. "Remember, we can only shoot you jumping into the pool once. Because once you're wet, you're wet and we don't have time for you to dry off, dry your clothes and reshoot. So don't mess up, all right?"

"Gotcha." Dylan walks back over to the band. I slip into the pool, and go under the water, getting my hair wet. Then I swim into position.

A second later, everyone's back in their places and the band is playing again, and then Dylan's playing his guitar, and then he takes the guitar off, leaves it on the pool deck and then looks at me. Right at me. Then he's jumping off the edge, into the pool. Ben points to me and I head underwater, thinking about how I'm going to hold my breath without looking like a blowfish. Why didn't I practice this ahead of time?

At first I can't see anything underwater but the bubbles from Dylan jumping in. But then the bubbles float to the surface and Dylan's there, swimming toward me. He grabs me by the waist and pulls me close. The water is stinging my eyes but I don't even blink because I don't want to miss a second of this. Or kiss his nose by mistake. But before I can really overthink it, his lips are on mine. And then a second later, we're swimming up, in synch, and breaking the surface. I sputter for breath, and so does he. The music is still playing and I look around and everyone is still splashing around like nothing's happened. I look back at Dylan and he looks at me and grins as the music fades out.

"All right all right," Ben yells. "We've got it. That's a wrap."

Dylan and I swim to the edge. He pulls himself out of the water first, then helps me out. "Thanks for that," he says, his dimple showing, and I look into his eyes, wondering if he might kiss me again, for real. But someone's grabbing my elbow.

"Hey, your phone is going crazy," Dace whispers and hands me my phone to me.

I stare at my screen. Two missed calls—both from Mom. Plus a text: Call me.

She knows. I grab my towel and move to a quieter part of the pool deck, Dace by my side.

"I know you didn't go to the dentist," Mom says when she answers, without saying hi. "So before you make up another lie, come straight home."

"OK," I say quietly then hang up. "Did you hear that?"

"Eek. Yeah."

"What am I going to tell her I was doing?"

Dace looks over at me. "The truth? What do you have to lose?"

•   •   •

Mom's sitting at the kitchen table, sorting through papers when I come in. She looks up, unsmiling.

"Do you want to go first or do you want me to?" she says.

"I'm not sure it totally makes a difference?" I say, preparing for the worst. "But, um, sure, you?"

"OK. So here's what my day was like. I was at work thinking about how soon you'll be gone and on your own and how little time left we have together, where I can just be your mom and take you to the dentist, so I convinced Terry to cover my shift and I went to the dentist to meet you. But you weren't there. And the receptionist was surprised to see me, because neither of us were scheduled for an appointment. So then I thought, you must have got the day wrong, but no, you weren't scheduled for an appointment at all this week, or next week or even the week after. And then I still had this thought like maybe you had just heard the voicemail wrong. But she never left you a message. And I called you, and you didn't answer. Do you know how worried I was? And I realized I was being duped by my own daughter. Do you know how stupid I felt? Why did you lie to me? Is that the kind of relationship we have?"

"Dylan was doing a music video," I blurt. "They were shooting it at the water park. And he asked me to be in it. With Dace. You would've said no."

"Pippa, you're 17. You've been accepted into your dream college. Why would I tell you that you can't miss one day of senior year?"

I just stare at Mom, not sure what to say next.

"You do recall that I was your age once, right?"

My stomach feels like there are rocks in it. If she only knew the truth.

"Come here," Mom says, standing and opening her arms wide. I walk toward her. "I don't like it when you lie to me. It makes me feel like I can't trust you." She sighs.

"I'm sorry."

"I hate that you'd ever think we're on two different teams. I'm on your team. Just talk to me."

"OK," I say, but I feel sick. Is now my moment to tell her just how many colossal lies I've been telling her? I don't know how to start . . .

But she gives me a peck on the cheek and moves to grab her purse. "I have to go to a meeting at the bank. But I'll pick up a pizza for us for tonight?" And I remember that it's Friday and our night. Well, it's supposed to be our night. But Hank has some Corvette Club event, so Charley's sleeping over. For once, I'm relieved to have the pint-sized distraction.

●　●　●

Skip ahead four hours and it's Mom, Charley, me, a pizza and the *Gilmore Girls*. I'm trying to track the rapid-fire dialogue while Charley asks about a billion questions and I try not to lose my patience with him. Between episodes Mom gets up to get us more soda.

"Aren't you getting tired, Charley?" I ask.

He gives me a look. "My dad said I could stay up as late as I wanted. Or that if I do fall asleep, I can just sleep in your room because it's going to be my room anyway when you go to college."

"*What?*"

"We're going to move in, and I can choose my room." He rearranges the sleeping bag on himself and grins at me.

My heart drops about a foot into the pit of my

stomach. Mom's planning to let Hank move in when I'm gone? And Charley knows before me? But if that's the case, why would Mom need a mortgage?

Mom returns carrying three glasses and places them on the coffee table. And I don't know what to do.

"Pippa, are you going to hit play?" Mom asks. So I do and fold my arms over my chest, staring at the screen and trying to push all other thoughts out of my head, but even *Gilmore Girls* is against me. Rory has always wanted to go to Harvard. But now, Lorelai finds out that Rory also applied to Yale, her grandfather's alma mater. Her mom is upset that she never told her that she even applied to Yale.

Even Rory had a backup plan.

After the episode ends, Mom turns to me. "One more?"

Charley's finally asleep at the end of the couch.

"Sure," I say. Maybe Rory'll rescind her application or not get into either school, or something that will make me feel slightly better about my own life.

"I'm just going to put the leftover pizza in the fridge." When Mom returns, she has a puzzled look on her face. "Hey, I meant to ask you—Reba, you know that woman in my Pilates class? Her daughter goes to Concord, and she got accepted to the same program you applied to at Brown. So shouldn't you have heard too, if they're sending out acceptances?"

I pretend to yawn, stretching my arms above my head. "I don't know. Maybe they send it out by school or something. Or maybe she got early acceptance."

"Well, I think you should check with your guidance counselor or call the college. What if there was a glitch?"

"What difference does it make?" I say, shifting away from her on the couch.

"You did all that work to apply, you should at least know if you got in or not. In case you change your mind about Tisch."

"Change my mind? Why on earth would I change my mind?"

Mom holds her hands up. "OK, OK." She's using that voice she used to use when I was throwing a temper tantrum. "Calm down. Of course you may never change your mind. It's just—you know I thought I was always going to be a model. And I did it, as hard as it was—moved to New York, not knowing a soul, living in a house full of models, not even knowing how to cook for myself or do my own laundry. I never thought about a backup plan, or what I'd do *after* modeling. I didn't think about the what-ifs. Like what if I got pregnant, and my boyfriend didn't want to be with me and I had to move back home again."

"Yeah, but things worked out. Dad came with you."

"Yes, he did. And I always loved him for that. But I couldn't model anymore, not here, in Spalding. My modeling career was over. Everything changed. And when Dad died, everything changed again. And I had to get a job—which is *not* my dream job— and work crazy hours. And not see you as much as

I want to, and I wonder, What if I had taken some classes, while I was in New York, gone to college part-time with the money I was making modeling? Or maybe when you had started grade school, if I had taken a course or two, gotten a degree in something. Then when I really needed it, I could've put that skill to use. But I don't have a skill. All I have is a job with crappy pay and a lot of hours. And I do it. Because that's what you do when life throws you for a loop. You buckle up and you just hold on and you do it. But *you*, Pippa, you don't have to just do it. You love photography, and you're great at it. But what if you grow out of it, then what? All your schooling will be in photography; all your eggs are in one basket. So if you ever change your mind, or you can't find work as a photographer, then what? I just don't ever want you to feel stuck."

Mom looks at me, her eyes glassy. I stare down at the TV remote in my hand, willing myself not to cry.

"I'm sorry, Mom. I mean, I know you work so much and you don't love it, but you never complain. I should've been helping out more, earning money . . ." Is this why Hank and Charley are moving in? To save money?

"Pipsqueak, no. That's not what I meant," Mom says. "This isn't about the money. It's about keeping your options open. You're so young. And this is a big decision."

"Okay, I get it," I say, leaning back in the couch and closing my eyes.

"So I wanted to ask you something," Mom says.

"What?" I open my eyes.

"Well," Mom sighs, "you know Hank and I—well, things have been going so well . . ." And there it is. She's going to ask if I'm OK with Hank moving in, along with his son. Of course I don't get off scot-free for skipping school to be in a music video. This is my punishment. "Hank asked me to go away for the weekend. For our anniversary. Just overnight. We'd leave tomorrow and be back Sunday. We'd need you to babysit Charley, if you were up for that."

I don't know whether to be relieved that all she wants to do is go away, or that she's also not being totally truthful either.

"I'd just be a phone call away. And I think it would mean a lot to Charley. He really likes hanging out with you. It could be a real bonding moment for you two, without the parents around."

"Sure," I say, and I stand. "You know, I'm pretty tired."

"Oh," she says. "You sure you don't want to watch another?"

I shake my head. "Not tonight. I'm going to go to bed." While it's still my bed, in my bedroom, I think, as I head up the stairs.

"Your mom is going away and you didn't tell me?!" Dace calls me immediately after I text her in the morning. I've just gotten home from garbage picking and seen Mom and Hank off on their romantic getaway in the Ford Focus.

"I'm telling you now. She just told me last night right before I was going to bed."

"Ahh. Oldest trick in the parent book. The short-notice, casual mention about going away. They've probably had that getaway booked for weeks."

"Huh?"

"Parenting Rule #1. Never give your teenager notice that you're going away. That way there's no time to throw a party. She really underestimates our skills."

"I'm not throwing a party."

"Give me 24 reasons why not."

"I'll give you one—"

"Nope. I said 24. And you can't do it. How many times have you thrown a party when your mom wasn't home?"

"You know I never have."

Dace has thrown parties, and we've had our share of going to other people's parties when their parents are away, but throwing one myself?

"Exactly. Which makes this a must-do. Add it to the list. It's the perfect excuse to invite your McAlmost Boyfriend over. I'll be there in 20 minutes."

As promised, Dace shows up at my door less than half an hour later, weighed down by her massive backpack. "This thing is Kilimanjaring my back." She dumps it on the ground. "Party supplies," she explains as she stretches her arms over her head. "Wait a second," she says, looking past me to the kitchen, where Charley's sitting at the table, watching a show on his iPad. "What's Charlie Brown doing here?"

"Don't call me Charlie Brown," he says.

"Shhh." I put a finger to my lips. "See? I was trying to tell you this is why I can't have a party. Charley's sleeping here tonight."

"Fukushima." She exhales loudly. "We've got to get him out of here. It would be irresponsible of us to expose him to an evening of drinking and debauchery."

"Um, drinking and debauchery are not in the plan, actually. Can't we just have a normal Saturday Sleepover?" I say, locking the front door and following Dace into the kitchen.

"No way, San José. Hey buddy," she says to Charley, "who's your best friend?"

"José."

"Whoa. That was trippy," Dace says. "Does this mean I'm psychic? Ooh, what if I set up a psychic reading booth while we're traveling? How awesome would that be?" She turns back to Charley. "What's José's last name?"

Charley shrugs. "No idea."

"Any idea what his phone number is?"

"He's eight. He doesn't have a phone."

"Well, how do you get in touch with him?"

Charley holds up his tablet. "I text him on his iPad."

"Great—why don't you let him know you want to have a super fun sleepover at his house, tonight?"

●　●　●

But José turns out not to be in town, either. So Charley goes along with us as we go shopping for supplies (turns out Dace's enormous backpack really *is* handy). Next we create several drink stations with soda and ice and set up a bunch of blow-up chairs in my backyard to encourage people to spend time outside, not in. But just in case they do come in, we move all breakables and valuables from the main floor. Then the doorbell rings.

I answer it to find a delivery guy.

"You ordered the popcorn machine?" he says.

Dace pushes past me. "Yes, yes I did." She turns to me and smiles. "All parties need popcorn machines, right?"

"Yes, they do!" Charley cheers, clapping his hands.

Finally, Dace says it's time to invite people.

"Should we make a list?" I ask.

"I don't think that's necessary," Dace says. "I think basically you should open up your texts and invite everyone on the list. You know, aside from your mom and Hank."

I consider inviting Gemma and Emma first, but instead text Dylan.

While I'm texting the 17th person in my contacts, Dylan texts back.

Dylan: Is there a theme? Like grunge or disco?

Me: Um, no.

Dylan: So you're saying don't wear purple PVC?

Me: I think it might be overkill.

Dylan: K. Working show tonight so it'll be pretty late. How late's too late?

Dace peers over my shoulder. "Tell him the party doesn't start till he walks in. And then get back to inviting people so this is actually a party and not you and me and a bucket of popcorn."

My heart's pounding as I text back. Dylan's coming to my house. My parent-free house. Where we might potentially kiss again. Above water.

"Come on," Dace says after we've invited everyone we know. "Time to change."

"I thought this looked pretty good," I say, running my hands over my black jeans as I follow her. I'm wearing a black halter top that I love, and the all-black thing works on me.

"You look like Darth Vader," Charley says, following us up the stairs.

"I've been telling her that for months," Dace says. "I brought half my closet. Just have a look."

She's not kidding. There's a huge heap of clothes on the floor of my room.

"What's this?" Charley asks, dangling one of Dace's thongs.

"A lasso," says Dace, taking it back and stuffing it in her pocket.

We set Charley up with *Star Wars Rebels* downstairs, and upstairs in my room, Dace gets down on her knees and starts rummaging through the pile and tossing items at me, then instructing me to swap them for something else. "We're getting closer." She tosses a red and blue striped bikini at me. "Here, put this on."

"Umm, I don't have a pool," I remind her.

"Details, shmetails. This makes you seem summery. It's just your base layer anyway, instead of underwear. Just trust me. It lets you have more freedom with your next layers because you're technically already wearing clothes."

"This is too weird," I say, stripping down until I'm naked, then pulling on the bikini. I wrap my arms around my waist.

Next she hands me a brightly striped flowy dress that I pull over my head. She pulls the sleeves down. "It's supposed to be off the shoulder." She stands back and nods.

I check my appearance in the mirror. "It's kind of see-through."

"It's *sheer*. See how the bikini came in handy?"

I turn around in the mirror. I do look cute. "What if he doesn't come?" I say, feeling nervous.

"He's going to come. He said he was going to come. OK, so Ben's going to bring beer—"

"You talked to Ben?" Dace's face reddens, and I cock my head. "You're blushing."

"I'm not."

"You *are.*"

"I may have run into him the other day."

"OK—"

"And we grabbed coffee."

"Like, a coffee *date*?" I say.

"Never mind Ben. Let's talk about Dylan. Have you talked about the text you never answered? The breakup?"

I shake my head. "No. You know, before, I felt like he was a slacker, and I had all these life goals. But now it's like the roles are reversed. He's at Harvard, and I'm, like, nowhere. What if he feels the way about me that I used to feel about him?"

"Uh, no way. I saw the kiss on the playback monitor. He's not an actor. You're not an actor. And there were *serious sparks*. Fireworks, really."

"Fireworks?" I say hopefully.

"Fourth of July kind of fireworks."

"Being in love is so gut-wrenching."

"Yes, but it also makes you feel *alive*."

●　●　●

By 8:30, just when I'm starting to worry that no one's going to actually come to my party, Gemma and Emma and a bunch of other girls arrive. We've dimmed the lights wherever we could, and Charley's put out a bunch of glow sticks and bracelets. I've even made him a Shirley Temple—7UP, grenadine, OJ and a little drink umbrella. Dace brought over the mini lights she usually has strung over her canopy bed, and we've strung them in the backyard.

"Welcome cocktail?" Dace asks the girls, and they all accept. I fill up five Solo cups with the concoction Dace and I created and hand them out as Ben arrives with a couple of guys who went to Spalding last year, carrying cases of beer. Dace and I wanted to have a signature drink because it seemed very un-high-school party of us, but we were limited to what Dace could swipe from her basement: a bunch of bottles of sparkling wine that her mom had left over from a baby shower she'd hosted, plus an almost-full bottle of vodka. So we threw them all in a jug with some lemonade and are calling it a Spring Fling. It's pretty good, IMO.

"What *is* this?" Emma says, her eyes widening after taking a sip.

"Spring Fling!" I say a little too loudly as the front door opens and a bunch of juniors storm in. I wonder if we should've put a sign on the front door telling people to go around to the backyard. I'm starting to worry that my plan to get people outside is not going to go very smoothly.

"I never thought you would throw a party!" Gemma practically hollers as someone turns up the music on the sound dock in the kitchen.

"Yeah, me either," I say as the door opens and more people stream in. No Dylan, just randoms. Ben returns from the kitchen and slings an arm around Dace. *Huh.* "I had to take some stuff out of your fridge to fit the beer in," Ben says. "You know, like, vegetables. I shoved them in the pantry by the cereal, OK?"

I make a mental note to get any traces of lettuce and snap peas out of there before Mom finds them, but things are already starting to feel a bit fuzzy and I wonder if I better switch to plain old lemonade? But Dace was right: throwing a party is something the old Pippa never would've done. I would've been too worried nobody would come, and look, I think, the house is packed. I snap pics as everyone's having a great time. Everyone has a Solo cup. Including Charley. "Charley!" I yelp. "What's in that cup?" I taste it—and, luckily, it checks out fine. 7UP.

After heading to the kitchen to refill my drink (turns out, all the lemonade is in the Spring Fling), I walk around, catching bits and pieces of other people's conversations, taking group selfies. When my cup is empty, I refill and find Dace and Ben and my other friends in the living room, and sit down beside Dace on the sofa. We play Would You Rather? (the drinking version) for a bit, then talk turns to summer plans.

"You guys should totally buy your Eurail passes soon," Gemma says, and then goes off on a whole spiel about her vacation last summer with her cousin, but I'm watching Dace. How do I tell her I can't afford to go?

"We don't need to buy them *right* now," I say, trying to move the conversation on.

"Yeah, Dace's gonna work with me at White Water World," Ben says, taking a swig of his beer. He puts his arm around her bare shoulders. She's wearing a white off the shoulder peasant-style dress that gives her skin a golden glow.

"You are?" I say, realizing this could solve all my problems.

Dace gives Ben a look and twists out from under his arm. "No. I'm not. He's dreaming. Besties before the resties. Sorry, Big Ben. Pip and I have plans."

"But Pippa could work at the water park too," Ben says. "We already talked about it. Remember, Pip?"

I gulp my drink and let the alcohol burn the back of my throat. "Well, kinda. And I guess we *could* do that, actually." I say. "Make some money this summer."

"What the Helsinki, Pip," Dace says, throwing back her drink and slamming her cup on the ground beside her. "The *plan* is to backpack 'crosh Europe, remember?" she slurs. "Also, what do you need the money for? 'Snot like you have to pay for Tisch. You didn't get in."

Whoa. That was harsh.

"I didn't get in *yet*. And I don't have parents who can drop thousands on me to do whatever I want, like it's nothing. You don't get it. Rent and food and my tuition and . . . New York is expensive." But it comes out "expenshive."

"OK, let me get this straight," Dace says. "You're telling me now that you're not going on the best trip of your life because you have to save for a college you didn't get into? Just work when you get back. It's not like you'll even need money living at home next year."

Ben puts a hand on Dace's knee to get her to stop talking. She hasn't said anything I haven't thought a hundred times, but it's so much worse hearing it out loud. What if I don't get into Tisch and have to live in Spalding next year, with no plan, while everyone else moves away or moves on . . . Dace reaches over and grabs Ben's beer, takes a swig then points it at me.

"I'm just saying, we had a plan, Pippa. And you can't think only about yourself. My plans to travel next year are based on where we go in the summer. I've been researching my trip for months."

"Oh come on, Dace. You've memorized a bunch of landmarks and use them instead of swears. And I'm not stopping you from going. I just can't do it."

"Of course you can't. You're only thinking about yourself. As usual."

"Are you kidding me? I wouldn't even *be* in this predicament if I'd thought about myself this past year, instead spending every single Sunday for months with you. That's selfish?"

"I didn't ask you to come visit me. You don't get to lord that over me."

"Then don't say that I think only about myself. But yes, now? Maybe I am thinking about myself. So what if I don't want to take a slacker year?" The second the phrase leaves my mouth I regret it.

"Slacker year? That's what I'm taking? That's what you think of me?"

"No. I—just. You know, your meditation word was *Be*. Mine was *Succeed*. We're just on *different* paths."

"I'm on a flaky path of privilege, and you're such a driven artiste. That's what you mean."

"I didn't say that."

"You didn't have to." Dace stands, dropping Ben's beer can. "You think I don't have ambition just because it's not like yours? But remember? I had a plan. And it didn't work out. My drive to *succeed* nearly killed me. But you're so self-absorbed you can't even see that other people's problems are just as valid as yours." Dace pushes her way out of the living room toward the front door.

I turn back to the group, all eyes on me. I try to say something but I can't focus on words that would make any sense at this point. Then I stand and run up the stairs, into my room.

"Hi Pippa," Charley says from where he's lying on my bed, still fully clothed, playing on his handheld video game device.

"Hey, want me to tuck you in?"

"Yeah," he says sleepily.

"Move over," I say, crawling onto the bed, and pulling the covers up over us.

"We're having a sleepover in my room . . ." he says, but my eyes close before I have a chance to correct him.

"Ohhhhhhhhhhhh . . ." Pain. My head is pounding. The room is too bright. My mouth, too dry. Sitting up triggers a wave of nausea. I lie back down again. The lemonade mimosas. The party. The fight with Dace.

Summoning the strength and the willpower, I roll over onto my side, wincing, and then swing my legs down to the ground and try to sit up again. Then stand. Another bad idea. I rush to the bathroom and make it just in time—if throwing up in the sink instead of the toilet counts as making it in time. I slide down the tile wall to the floor and try to bury my head in the fluffy floor mat.

I need to know what time it is. I splash my face with cold water and dry my face, gargle some mouthwash and then crawl back to my room to look around for my phone. I can't find it. I try to think back through the night, then remember that after the fight with Dace, I went to my room and passed out. I just left everyone to party in my house.

This is not good.

I pull myself up and head downstairs, bracing myself for what I know is going to look like post-party pandemonium.

But when I get to the bottom of the stairs, I stop. It's spotless. I look into the living room and every square inch of it is completely impeccable. Not a cup, chip or beer bottle anywhere to be seen. And then I notice someone on the couch. Faded jeans, gray T-shirt. Dylan. He looks up. Then sits up. Blue high-top Vans hit the floor as Dylan blinks a few times and looks around.

"Dylan?"

"Whoa." He rubs his face with his hands. "I must've fallen asleep."

Dylan never even came to the party. Did he?

"Did you clean up?"

"I figured you weren't going to be in any shape to clean this place up this morning. Despite your stellar garbage picking skills."

I sit down on the couch beside him, my shoulder brushing his. Tingles everywhere.

"It was pretty bad in here," he says. "Not gonna lie."

"Thank you." I put my head in my hands and lean forward.

"You feel that good, huh?"

"That's an understatement."

"Hang on." He gets up and heads to the kitchen,

and I realize I probably look as terrible as I feel. But at least I swigged that mouthwash. He returns a second later and hands me two Advil and a can of Coke. "Trust me on this. There's something in it that will magically make you feel better."

I take the Advil and open the can of Coke and take a swig.

He sits back down. "I'm guessing you haven't seen your Instagram?"

My small head shake hurts. "Can't find my phone." He pulls out his. A few clicks later he turns it to me.

My feed is full of drunken party pics. Some feature other people. Most are selfies of drunk me. Some of them have been in my feed for 10 hours. I posted these? Rubbing my eyes doesn't make the pics any less blurry, but the likes and comments are in focus. Dozens of likes. A bunch of comments. I spend hours setting up shots, creating themes, editing images, posting at scheduled times, and these shots only get a handful of likes and even fewer comments. Then I get wasted, take a bunch of terrible, poorly composed shots at the same party and post them all within a few hours and they do better than all my other photos combined? I groan. "So embarrassing."

He tilts his head. "You want my honest, totally pedestrian opinion?"

I shrug.

"These pics—sure they're not the *best* photos ever, but they're real. They're like the stuff you used to take pictures of. Real people, real emotions. You have this way of capturing people and really showing them. And somehow despite not being able to have any control over lighting, you managed to make these look good."

"Our house has really good lighting. My dad was pretty crazy about it, actually. I guess most photographers are. It's all about the dimmers."

Dylan gives me a dramatic eye roll. "Pippa, you have a great eye. Even when you're wasted. It's not about the dimmers."

"Anyway," I say, looking around. "I can't believe you cleaned everything up for me. It's, like, cleaner than it was before the party. As if you'd do all this for an ex-girlfriend."

"I was kinda hoping we could get rid of that 'ex' status," he says, shifting his body and wrapping his arm around me. I lean into him. "Come here," he says, and we nestle in together on the couch, our bodies spooning.

"I missed you, Philadelphia Greene," he says.

"Me too." I barely manage to get it out. We lie there, and I listen to his steady breath, letting my eyes close.

● ● ●

"Pippa?"

I open my eyes and see Mom standing in the entrance to the living room. It takes me a minute to clue in, and then it all comes rushing back.

I jolt upright, flinging Dylan's arm off me. "Mom!" I say too loudly, standing up and realizing I'm still in my see-through-dress-over-bikini ensemble.

"What's going on?" she says, just as Hank comes in the door, carrying their overnight bags.

Mom looks from Dylan to the front door, where I notice the garbage bags piled up in the entranceway. In particular, the clear bag packed with beer cans, vodka bottles and Solo cups.

Mom pulls her hair back off her face, the way she does when she's really upset, and then says, "Hello, Dylan."

"Hi Mrs. Greene," Dylan says, standing. "I should go. Um, I'm sorry?"

Hank stares at me. "Where's Charley?" I've never seen his eyes so wide. His voice is filled with panic.

My stomach drops. It's a good question. Among all the other stuff I've done, I've lost Hank's son?

Dylan saves me again. "He's up in your bedroom, Mrs. Greene. Watching *Big Hero 6* on his tablet." Then Dylan gives me a small wave and slips out the front door.

"This is what you do the one time I leave you alone?" my mom says quietly. "You have a party?"

"I'll take Charley home," Hank says. He seems to be frozen, probably paralyzed with the thought that this is what his life is going to be like when he moves in.

"That's a good idea," Mom says. "Because we have quite a lot to talk about, Pippa. Starting with explaining to me why you didn't tell me that you got waitlisted."

I'm pretty sure my heart stops beating for a minute. "Hank told you?"

"Hank didn't tell me anything."

Hank bends down to pick up Charley's shoes. "Charley, let's go," he hollers upstairs. "Holly, call me . . . later." After an awkward minute where no one says a word, Charley's sneakers are on and they're out the door.

Mom turns back to me. "What on Earth possessed you to lie to me about Tisch?"

"I didn't mean to," I say. Head really pounding now, I sink down onto the couch. "I meant to tell you right away, and you didn't answer your phone, so I texted you and it autocorrected. And then you thought I got in. I swear. And I didn't want to let you down, and I thought I could fix it myself."

"And the trip to New York? What was that?"

"I went to try to convince the program coordinator to let me in."

"Why didn't you just *tell* me that?" Mom says, her voice softening. Her eyes examine my face, as though the answer is written there in cryptic code.

"I don't know." I feel a lump forming in my throat, and I try to swallow, but no go. "It all got so out of hand."

"Sounds like it. Honestly, Pippa, I feel like I'm looking at someone I don't even know." She sighs and I feel it: her disappointment.

"I'm so sorry." I get up and walk toward her, expecting her to hold out her arms and hug me the way she always does when we fight. But she doesn't. She folds her arms across her chest.

"I need to think through all of this, Pippa."

I stand in silence, wondering what to do next. She turns and goes into the kitchen. I walk toward the stairs, then stop. She knows about the waitlisting, and the party, but there's still one last lie. "Mom?"

She turns to face me, one hand on the kitchen table. "Hmm?"

"I didn't apply to any other colleges. That's why I haven't heard back from anywhere but Tisch."

She stares at me without saying anything, and so I wait, until finally, she shakes her head, slowly. "Wow."

I didn't think it was possible to feel any worse than I did when I woke up this morning, but I was wrong. Turns out disappointment trumps a hangover any day.

●　●　●

I stay in my room, skipping dinner, which isn't exactly a sacrifice since even the whiff of barbecued chicken I'm getting through my open window is making me dry-heave. But I'm dying for a ginger ale, so eventually I slip downstairs. Mom and Hank are in the yard, their backs to the house, sitting in Adirondack chairs, two glasses of wine on the little table between them. The sun is setting, and I can hear Mom laughing at something Hank is saying. Charley's kicking a soccer ball against the fence. I can see why Mom would want Hank to live with her—with us. He makes her happy. And when I do move out, whether it's in the fall or whenever, she *will* be lonely. Do I really want her to be all alone, just because I don't want to give up my childhood bedroom?

I reach into my pocket for my phone, remember I still can't find it, go upstairs, grab my camera out of the bottom drawer of my desk and go back downstairs, quietly open the sliding door and take a few shots of Mom and Hank together. No rule of thirds, no leading lines, just the two of them, the setting sun lighting the shot. Giving it the golden hour glow.

Charley catches my eye and waves, then runs inside. "You wanna watch a show together?"

"Sure. What do you want to watch?" I ask, bracing myself for an episode of *Star Wars Rebels*. But instead he says *Gilmore Girls*.

"No-go on *Gilmore Girls*. Can't watch it without my mom. Let's pick a show just for us."

"Yeah!" Charley says, following me downstairs. I smile. He's not the *worst*.

Monday can't come soon enough, but when I wake up I feel worse than yesterday. Is it possible to be *more* hungover on Day 2 than Day 1? No clue, but I drag myself out of bed and out the door to school before Mom wakes. Dace and I haven't spoken to each other, and I'm nervous about seeing her at our lockers. When I get to school, a bunch of people tell me how fun the party was and want to know if I got busted for having a party. I answer their questions as breezily as I can, trying to be cool. I don't see Dace, and I remember it's Monday Morning Meditation. There's no way I can go in there, so I head back outside and down the field behind the school to one of the large oak trees. Positioning myself so I'm out of sight, I sit cross-legged and put my hands on my knees like Anisha did. I close my eyes and think of a one-word mantra to get me through the practice.

But the only thing that comes to mind is *Regret*. And nausea.

● ● ●

In Writer's Craft, we get to choose our own word for the writing prompt, so I stick with my word of the day. Regret for how insensitive and cruel I was to Dace, regret that I've been lying to Mom, that I've let Dad down about Tisch. When Mr. Jonescu dings the bell, I've filled four pages of my notebook.

I grab the hall pass and head to the bathroom. Pushing open the door, I walk straight into Dace. For the first time since she got it, she's not wearing her backpack. Instead, a cute paisley cross-body bag is slung across her chest.

"Oh thank god." Dace pulls me in for a quick hug.

"I looked for you everywhere this morning. I couldn't find you and I had this terrible thought like, What if you died of alcohol poisoning and I just left you? Why haven't you replied to any of my texts? Turns out being worried trumps being pissed off."

"Sorry. Also I can't find my phone. Ever since the party. I've looked everywhere but it's MIA. Karma, I guess." I moan. "I also feel like crap. Is it possible to be hungover for this long?"

"Doubtful. You're probably just dehydrated and stressed out."

"Stressed out about—" and then I remember. My driver's test. "Oh no. No no no no no."

"You *forgot*?"

"My life is in my phone! Yes I forgot! I can't take

it. I'm not mentally prepared. I didn't even ask Mom if I could borrow her car. You have to take it for me."

"I am pretty sure it doesn't work that way. Maybe for Emma and Gemma, but not for us." Dace wraps her arm around me. "I'll take you after school. And you can use my car."

"Really?"

"You think I want to be driving you around when you're 80?"

I turn to hug her, though mostly I'm hanging off her. "I'm sorry I said you were a slacker. I didn't mean it. You're not a slacker at all. I think I'm probably just jealous that you do *have* a plan, and it's super fun."

"It's OK," she says. "I don't want to just go to college and waste my parents' money when I don't even know what I want to do. I'm not like you. I don't have a forever dream."

"Yeah, well, you did."

"Yeah, I did. And you still do. You're just having a hiccup."

I break away from Dace and rush into one of the stalls. While I spend some up close and personal time with the toilet, Dace distracts me with gossip from the party that we missed because we were too busy concentrating on our cocktails and bickering.

Eventually I emerge, feeling slightly better, and Dace helps me clean myself up, then passes me a water bottle from her bag. "You can keep it."

As we walk down the hall, I fill her in on everything—Dylan, my mom and that David was the one who told my mom about me not getting into Tisch.

"Blah blah blah back to Dylan. You know he got a show, right?"

"What?"

"Opening for the Cherry Blasters. Wednesday night."

"Why didn't he—" and then I remember my missing phone. "We'll go?"

Dace bites her lip. "Ben and I sort of made plans for Wednesday night because he's not working. But obviously I can cancel. You have to go."

"Yeah, but you don't. Don't cancel on Ben. All the more reason to get my license, right?"

• • •

Dace pulls into the DMV and pops her Fiat into a spot near the building. I really should've been driving here from school, to actually practice driving her car, but a wave of nausea made me decide to take the passenger seat one more time. "Listen," she says, "I don't want to bring up the Big V, but I need to."

"My virginity? I don't think now is the time to talk about my sex life."

"*Vomit.* I love you, but if you vomit in my car, you're going to have to look for a new best friend."

She hands me the keys and a small pink sparkly gift bag. "It's empty. Makeshift barf bag. Use it in an emergency."

The DMV is green and white inside, the plastic chairs we sit on are cold on my butt. Dace sits beside me, and a second later, Mom walks in and sits on the other side. "You didn't think I wasn't going to come and wish you good luck, did you?" I'd texted Mom earlier from Dace's phone, to remind her why I wouldn't be home straight after school.

A few minutes later, a grandfatherly looking man wearing khakis and a bright green Polo shirt calls my name. "Frankly," he says, shaking my hand. His hair is graying at the temples, and he has a kind face and those crinkly lines at the eyes that make you look like you're smiling even when you're not. I wait for him to continue. He doesn't.

"Sorry, what?" I say.

"First name Frank. Last name Lee. Ha ha, I know, my name is hilarious."

One foot in front of the other, Pippa. Breathe in, breathe out. Don't puke. I can do this. The SATs may have been a flop the first time around. I might be waitlisted for Tisch. But flu or not, I am passing this test.

Once we're both in Dace's car with our seatbelts on, I check that all my mirrors are in the right place and then start the car. For the next 20 minutes, Frank Lee gives me commands and I do as he says. Things go pretty well until he says, "Three-point turn."

I stare at the road behind me in the rearview mirror. It seems narrower than it should. I want to ask him if we can just turn onto another street.

"There's a car behind me," I say.

"There are going to be cars on the road when you're driving."

My heart is pounding. My mouth feels dry.

The car behind me honks. Frank Lee puts his

hand out the window and gestures for the guy to go around me.

"All right, there you have it," Frank Lee says. "No cars on the road."

I take a deep breath and look around and then turn the wheel to the left and press the gas pedal. I stop just before the curb. Check all my mirrors and blind spots, crank the wheel right, reverse, then straighten out. I did it.

"Turn left at the light," Frank Lee commands, "and park back at the DMV." A wave of nausea consumes me as I pull up to the intersection. The red light gives me a nanosecond to breathe deeply and pray I make it through the rest of the test. The light changes and I inch into the intersection and wait to turn as cars zip past. The light turns yellow, as another car approaches. He slows and I turn the wheel, only then noticing that he's speeding up. I'm not sure what to do: stop, or hit the gas and pray he doesn't hit me. The gas pedal practically touches the ground and we're through the intersection in the clear. I focus on the road, only then realizing that for the first time all day I haven't felt sick. Not much of a consolation given I probably just flunked my test.

Back at the DMV, I put the Fiat in park.

"Well. It was a little more excitement than I normally get, but you have good instincts and you're a confident driver. Congratulations," Frank Lee says. "See you on the road."

And minutes later, I have my license. And the Fiat's still a barf-free zone.

On Tuesday morning I wake up early, get out Mom's favorite cookbook, its pages worn and wrinkled from spills, and turn to one of the dog-eared pages in the middle of the book: Mom's famous waffle recipe, her notes in the margins. They don't turn out as well as when Mom makes them on account of the fact that I'm a pretty terrible cook and we only have one egg in the fridge so I improvise with mayonnaise, which is supposed to be a substitute for egg, but I'm not totally sure it works. They taste a little tangy, but I figure it's the thought that counts, and there's always cereal as backup.

"What's this?" she says, rubbing her face when she comes into the kitchen. Things are definitely less chilly—Mom couldn't exactly let an event like me getting my driver's license go by without making a bit of a big deal—but we're still acting weird.

"Your famous waffles."

"It's not Sunday."

"I know, and they're also not as good as yours. Let's just call them apology waffles? They're also kind of burnt."

"Oh sweetie." She puts an arm around me and gives me a half smile. "Is there coffee?"

"Yes. Except I lost count on scoops. It's very strong."

"I never mind."

I pour her a cup and hand it to her.

She takes a sip. "Perfect. So, who wants to go first?"

"I think I better. So first—and these are in chronological order, not order of sorry-ness—I'm sorry that I lied about applying to other schools, which why did I even lie to you about that? And I'm sorry I didn't correct the autocorrect about getting into Tisch, or tell you why I really went to New York. And I'm sorry if I made things weird by asking Hank to keep my secret. And I'm sorry about the party, and skipping school." I take a breath. "I got myself into this whole mess and I felt like I had to get myself out, and I didn't want to confide in you about any one thing because then I'd confide about everything and you'd be so disappointed in me, just like Dad must be so disappointed in me. I couldn't take it. At least with my lies, you were proud of me, even if it was unwarranted. I wanted to fix it."

"Oh Pipsqueak," Mom says, putting down her coffee and wrapping her arms around me.

"Does this mean you forgive me?" I whisper when we pull apart.

"Yes, of course. That's not to say I'm not angry with you. It was stupid not to apply to any other colleges. This is your life. The future is scary and the unknown is scary, but sometimes being scared is a good thing."

"I guess."

"And I definitely think when you're already making bad choices and hiding them, adding a party, where you and everyone you know—or don't know—is drinking underage is a terrible idea. And having Charley at the party . . ."

"I know."

Neither of us says anything for a minute.

"That said, I think this is a tough time for you, and maybe I didn't check in with you enough, to see how you were doing. To give you a chance to talk to me." She puts her arms out and I let her hug me again. "We're going to figure this out."

"OK," I say, into her robe. "But I can't really breathe."

She pulls away from me and laughs. And I laugh too, tears in my eyes.

After breakfast I ask Mom if she wants to walk to school with me. "I know it's kind of pointless, because then you have to walk back home again. But—"

"I'd love to. Let me get dressed."

"Do you want to walk along the water?" Mom asks as we're walking down our street toward Waverly. "I know you always like that route for taking photos."

"Sure. I'm not really taking photos much anymore."

"I noticed. I guess that was sort of a leading comment. Why aren't you?"

I fill her in about the Vishwanathan meeting.

"But you love photography."

"I know. That's the problem. I'm supposed to be finding other things to do, but so far, I haven't found anything else I'm any good at."

We turn onto the path that leads down to the water. It's a sunny morning, one of those mornings where you can tell it's going to be really warm. I take off my black jean jacket but my black T-shirt and black jeans soak up the sun. "You know," Mom says, "I'm not sure you have to succeed at whatever you try in order to prove to Tisch that you have other interests. Maybe you just have to *try*. Maybe it's the journey, not the destination kind of thing."

"I never really thought about that. You know, *succeed* was my one-word mantra in Monday Morning Meditation."

"Monday Morning Meditation? How much of your life have I missed?"

"I only went once. And I got kicked out for taking pics on my phone. Definitely not a success."

"You know I choose a word to live by each year."

"You do? How do I not know this?"

Mom shrugs, and then pulls off her sweater and ties it around her waist. "It seemed corny, I guess."

"What's your word?"

"*Brave.* I figured, the last year you're living at home was a good year to be brave."

"Oh Mom," I say, "but you're always brave."

She gives a light laugh. "I don't feel it. Most of

the time I feel lost. You know for a long time I was a mom and a wife and I was really happy. And then Dad died, and now you're going to college, or not, or whatever"—she holds up her hands—"no pressure." She grins. "But eventually you'll move away from home. Then it might just be me. And what will *I* have to do?"

"But you have Hank. I thought . . . you two were moving in together."

She gives me a funny look. "No. What would make you think that?"

"Charley said he was taking over my room. And then I saw the mortgage application so I didn't know what to think. Was that . . . to pay for me to go to college? Because I didn't get a scholarship?"

Mom twirls her hair, then flicks it away. "Not exactly. I was just . . . looking at options. I want you to have the best opportunities and I don't want you to be in debt for the rest of your life to get them."

"Yeah, but you can't go into debt for me."

"Yes, actually, I can. It's called being a parent. Anyway, I'm sorry I worried you."

"I was thinking maybe I shouldn't go backpacking in July with Dace. Like, maybe I could get a job instead. Ben said he can probably get me hired at White Water World."

"Let's think about it. And *talk* about it."

We approach the edge of the school grounds, and I turn to Mom. "We should do this more often."

"Yeah," Mom says, hugging me. "We should." She turns to head home, then stops. "Oh. I can't believe I forgot to give this to you," she says, pulling my phone out her purse. "I found this in the backyard—the screen was smashed so I took it in to get fixed yesterday. Seems like you've been missed. Not that I was looking at your messages but it's been making a lot of noise." Mom's put one of those massive black waterproof cases on my phone. She hands it to me.

"Thanks, Mom."

Mom heads back in the direction we just came from, and I look at my phone. There's a bunch of texts from Dace, and one from David checking in on me, but my eyes jump to Dylan's.

Dylan: You OK?

Dylan: Call me when u can.

Dylan: If you're reading these texts but don't feel like replying, press 1.

Dylan: Maybe your fingers are broken. All of them. Could you use your chin to let me know?

Dylan: Or your nose?

Dylan: OK I'm just going to assume you're on a technology break and this has nothing to do with me.

Dylan: I got you a photo pass for my show. RFBR is playing on Wednesday night. I want you to come.

Dylan: If you're a big fat hairy dude who's found this phone and is reading all these texts, I do not have a photo pass for you.

Dylan: This is getting weird. I'm going to stop texting now.

Dylan answers on the first ring.
"I've never shot a concert before."
"Is that a yes?"
"It's a yes."

"You're not on the list. And the pit is full. Sorry. Next." The guy with the clipboard, manning the Will Call booth for media, looks past me to the next photographer in line. Someone bumps me from behind.

"Wait. No, I'm here for RFBR. The opener." The nervous lump in my throat seems to be growing by the minute.

Clipboard dude scribbles something on his clipboard. "Oh. All right. It won't be busy for the opener. But you need to come back right here"—he points to a random spot in the foyer—"before the Cherry Blasters go on and hand your pass back."

I clear my throat. "Of course."

He hands me a lanyard with a laminated pass and then points me toward a group of legit photographers, and I realize that I am likely the only one here who has never shot a concert before. My legs are wobbly, but I make my way over to the group.

In the corner of the entranceway, next to the black metal doors that lead into the venue, I lean against the wall and go over David's instructions from this afternoon when I called him to ask advice on shooting a concert: ISO 1600, a shutter speed of 1/160th and an aperture of f2.8. David said by putting the settings as low as possible I'd reduce the risk of having to adjust the settings in the dark and making a mistake, or missing a good shot because I wasn't ready.

"You're new, huh?"

I turn to face a girl with shiny black hair, the ends tinted purple. Freckles dot her nose. She's wearing a plaid shirt and cut-off jean shorts, with black high-tops.

"It's that obvious?" I say.

"Nah, just that we all work the same shows. You get to know a face. Also, I like how you don't feel the need to wear all black either." She nods at my light-wash jeans and grey sweater.

I laugh. "I'm Pippa."

"Jaime."

"Who are you shooting for?"

"I'm with *Rotate*."

"Wow. I love that site."

"Yeah, it's great." She pushes her sleeves past her elbows.

"So is this your full-time job?"

"Pretty much. I do this, some weddings and work as a waitress to make sure I can pay my rent when photography's slow. What about you?"

"I'm still in high school." The words come out before I realize there could be repercussions for admitting that.

She whistles. "Using your camera to sneak into a 21-and-over show, huh?" Is she going to tell on me? Then she smiles. "I used to do that too."

Someone shouts up ahead and the line starts to move. Not all the photographers follow Clipboard Dude—most are waiting for the Cherry Blasters, not interested in shooting three songs of an unknown opener's set, Jaime explains. "But I always shoot the opener. You never know who might make it big, you know?" I nod and follow her into the theater, staying in line, and stopping so there's about a foot between us. I pull my camera up to my face, wishing I'd checked the settings one more time before coming out, but it's too late, I've got to hope for the best. It's only when I'm standing there, the venue in near-darkness, the only sound that of the excited crowd, that I realize I've been so focused on getting here, getting in, and getting myself ready to take pictures, that I haven't focused on the fact I'm about to see Dylan. Onstage. Performing. To a massive crowd.

And then the stage lights go up. The screen hanging at the back of the stage is illuminated, and the RFBR emblem—the same one that's on the front of the drummer's kit—is projected onto the screen. Then the guitarist, drummer and bass player emerge from the left side of the stage. They make their way across the stage to their instruments, and a split second later, the speakers are pounding. And then Dylan walks out. Black jeans, gray T-shirt and a confident swagger. Hair swept to the side, stubble on his chin. He scans the crowd, picks up his guitar and slings the strap over his head. I quickly look around to get my bearings, then slide the camera into place, seeing the stage through the viewfinder. Guitars jangling, the drums keeping a poppy beat. I start clicking away, focusing on Dylan first, closing in on his face as he sings in the microphone and sways to the music between verses. I don't move around too much for the first song; for the second song I try to get a wider lens on the band, to fit them all into the shot. I pull the camera away a few times to check the shots but then remember I don't have a lot of time, and put the camera back up to my face. I snap away but then the camera fails to shoot. I pull it away and check the screen. *Memory card full.* Has it been that long since I downloaded my photos?

I have two choices here—stop shooting or start erasing, but I don't have time to be selective with the shots. I skip to the oldest shots on the camera and start deleting, hoping I've saved everything to my computer. The second song ends. I'm not sure how many photos I've erased, but I've got to make the next ones count. There's only one song left in the three-song photo opp. As the drummer counts them in, the screen behind the band switches from their logo to a video—there's a wide shot of a pool and then I realize: it's *the* video. Camera in front of my face, I play with angles the best I can, to get both the band in the video and the live band together in the shot. Then I zoom in on Dylan and blur out the video for a few shots. And then I see myself. I'm there, in the video. And I zoom in, past Dylan, past the band, as video-Dylan jumps into the water and meets me, under the water. I snap a shot just as our lips meet. My camera beeps. *Memory card full.*

And then the song ends, and the guy beside me is nudging me out toward the door. I glance back up at the stage at the same time as Dylan looks down. Our eyes meet, and I smile.

"How do you think you did?" Jaime asks as we walk back through to the foyer.

I make a face.

"It's intense, huh?"

"Definitely."

"All right, I'll see ya around."

Clipboard Dude is beside me, hand out. "Pass." I pull the lanyard over my head and place it in his hand. He gives a half smile. "But you can go in there and see the rest of the show."

RFBR play another few songs and walk off the stage to the sound of real applause—not polite clapping, but killed-it applause. It has nothing to do with me, but my heart swells with pride.

A minute later, my phone buzzes.

Dylan: Meet me by the merch booth?

People jostle against each other as they make their way to the bar or the bathroom, but a few minutes later, Dylan grabs my arm, and pulls me over to the edge of the hallway.

"You were amazing," I tell him, knowing it sounds like a cliché, but it's also totally true.

"You get any good shots of me?" That dimple.

"Maybe," I tease, patting my camera, which is slung over my shoulder.

He puts an arm around my waist. "Come on, I've got a spot where we can watch the Cherry Blasters." He leads me down the hallway and up a set of stairs, holding my hand, then down a dark hallway. A second later, colored spotlights illuminate the stage in front of us. We're at the stage, hidden by a dark curtain. The band walks out on the stage, from the opposite side. "Pretty good vantage point, huh?"

I nod and quickly delete more old photos, then raise my camera to my face. For the next few songs, I move around a bit, focusing on the band, getting the best shots until my memory card is full again. I sling my camera back across my body and turn to him. "Thanks."

"For what?" Dylan's breath is hot in my ear.

"For tonight."

Dylan's hands move down to my hips, and he pulls me close to him. Then we're swaying together, to the music. Our bodies close. And we stay like that for the rest of the song, until it ends. As the band starts up their next song, Dylan turns me to face him, my body brushing his.

His hands move from my hips, up my body, to my face, and he's pulling me into him and our lips are pressing against each other, hot and damp from sweat. Finally we pull apart and I catch my breath.

"Do you know how long I've wanted to do that?" he says. "Kiss you, like that, for real?"

My voice catches in my throat.

And then he's kissing me again.

When we break apart, I smile. "Um, no. No clue. How long?"

"A long time."

An hour later we're heading out of the venue, when I hear someone call my name.

Jaime is out of breath, behind me. "Pippa. Someone stole my camera, in the bathroom. Which, I know, I'm such an idiot to even leave my camera on the counter, but I'm screwed. I have nothing and I've got to get a photo in to my editor tonight. I've already asked three other dudes but no one can or wants to share with me. Please say you'll sell me one of yours?"

"I didn't shoot the Cherry Blasters."

"Yes you did," Dylan interrupts.

I give him a look. "Not officially."

"But you got something?" Jaime says. I nod and turn my camera toward her, and she flips through the shots. "These'll do. Can I take three? I'll pay you what I would've made."

"And make sure I get a credit?"

She nods. "It's a deal."

I refresh *Rotate*'s website a billion times before bed, give up, then check again when I wake up. It's there. My photo. My name. I send the link out: to Dace, Dylan, Ramona, Ben, David. My phone rings.

"I thought 6 a.m. wasn't morning to you?"

"It's not—but my daughter gets a photo published? That's worth getting up for. Plus your text woke me up."

"Daughter, huh?" David's never called me his daughter.

But he avoids the question. "So you gonna tell me how you got your first credit?"

I fill him in.

"Well, good for you, Greene." He clears his throat. "Listen, I'm proud of you. Whatever happens. If this Tisch thing works out, great. 'Cause then I'm going to force you to see me once a week. At least. But if it doesn't and you want to come chill in the city for a bit, you can always stay with me. As long as you like."

"Thanks, David."

After we hang up, I head downstairs, where I can hear Mom making coffee. I show her my phone. The pic. My name. She wraps her arm around me. "Oh Pip. I'm so proud of you."

I feel proud of myself too.

At lunch, Lisa lines up behind me as I'm waiting in line for chicken nuggets. "Hey Lisa," I say, and she looks up from her notebook, where she's scribbling something.

"Hi," she huffs and then puts her head down.

"How's everything going?"

"How do you *think* things are going?" she says. "Devyn's taken over Streeters but now she's not writing her column. So now we're OK on photos but short on words. What a way to go out of this place."

"Listen, I'm sorry about bailing on the site." But even as I say it, it occurs to me that I haven't for a second missed doing Streeters. I missed taking pictures, but not the kind I was churning out for *Hall Pass* or Instagram or photo club.

I grab my chicken nuggets, two chocolate chip cookies and a bottle of water and pay using my student card. "Well, good luck," I say half-heartedly, and Lisa rolls her eyes at me.

●　●　●

In Writer's Craft that afternoon, the prompt is Time. I turn to a blank page, and at the top I write

Future. I stare at it for a minute and scrawl *What next?* And then think about next year. How I have no clue what's next for me. I'm still writing when Mr. Jonescu tells us the time is up. After class, I'm walking to my locker when I bump into Lisa again.

"You said you were short on articles, right?" I say.

Lisa rolls her eyes. "You have no idea."

My essay for Tisch is due in six days. Writing for *Hall Pass* could be a good way to work through some ideas before the deadline. "Would you want a personal essay? I know I'm not a writer, but I have stuff from Writer's Craft and, I don't know, it's probably not great, but I was thinking if I cleaned it up a bit maybe—"

"Yes, sure, great," Lisa says. "Send it to me."

"I still need to work on it."

"Fine. Send it by Sunday night."

I wake up early, but Mom's already downstairs drinking coffee at the kitchen table. "I'm going to go garage saling. You want to come?"

"You haven't been garage saling yet this spring."

"Time to fix that." I hold up my camera.

She stands. "I'm with you."

We head out to the end of our street, which is often where people post signs for garage sales, and I do my usual thing of taking a picture of all the sale signs, so it's easier to find them later. Then we head down Waverly to the first sale. Mom heads to the table of books, and I run my hands over the old dishes, thinking about the fall. Will I need my own plates if I'm living on my own? I pull my camera up to my face and take a shot of the plates, lined up. I look around for Mom to see if she's ready to go and see she's by the garage, talking to someone.

"Pippa, do you remember Eleanor McKeown?" The woman's she's talking to smiles at me. "She was one of the nurses who took such great care of your dad in the hospital."

I nod. Eleanor has this thick wavy orange hair and freckles all over. She would sit with Dad forever, and any time we needed anything, she would get it. She would bring me drinks, and she would explain what the doctors had said in a way that I understood. "I volunteered at the hospital last year," I say.

"Ahh," she says. "I retired last year. I miss the hospital. The early mornings and overnight shifts? Not so much." She smiles. "You look so much older than I remember."

I shrug. "I feel the same."

"You must be graduating from high school soon? This year?"

I nod.

"And then what do you have planned?"

"I'm—" and then I say it. "I'm not sure."

"Ah well, you'll figure it out. I remember your dad thinking you might be a lawyer or a detective."

"Uhhh, like Sherlock Holmes?" I say, thinking she must have me confused with someone else. "Dad knew I was going to be a photographer, like him."

She tilts her head, then shakes it. "No dear, Evan and I talked about your future a lot." She looks over at my mom, maybe seeking permission to keep going. "I think, when he knew that the end was near, it was so hard on him—thinking about how he wouldn't see you graduate from high school, wouldn't know what you'd go on to do, who you'd become." She glances to her left, where a woman has approached a table full of glassware, then winks at us. "I've got my eye on those sherry glasses. I better get over there before they're gone. It was lovely to see both of you."

"Eleanor's right," Mom says when it's just the two of us. "I hadn't thought about it that way, your photography. You threw yourself into it so wholeheartedly that I almost forgot a time when you weren't so focused on taking pictures. It wasn't always your passion."

"Of course it was," I retort.

She shakes her head. "No, you didn't have that same intensity before he died," Mom says, putting a strand of my hair behind my ear. "Oh sure, you were always interested, but it felt like you were interested in photography because he was. And then he left you his Nikon. And it's almost as though you needed to find a tie to him. Something to hold on to. It's not a bad thing. I think it probably is what helped you get through everything, but maybe it doesn't have to be *everything* anymore."

"You're just saying that because I didn't get into Tisch," I say. "You wouldn't be saying that if I had gotten accepted."

"Maybe," she concedes. "Maybe not."

I start down the driveway, onto the street, steps ahead of Mom. Is Mom right? I replay the timeline. I got the Canon for Christmas before he died, but it wasn't until after he died that I got serious about photography. What did I want to be when I grew up, back when I was 12, 14? Before everything changed? Did I only start dreaming of Tisch after he died? I kick at a stone with the toe of my sneaker and watch it rattle down the street.

And if Tisch hasn't been my forever dream, then is it *my* dream at all? Mom catches up to me but we walk in silence, past the next garage sale, Mom taking her cue from me. I just want to go home. But when we get to the end of our driveway, I stop.

"Do you mind if I just go off on my own for a bit?"

She looks surprised, but nods. Then she reaches out to grab my arm. "Honey, I think you're probably working through some stuff right now, but I want you to know, that this time of your life—trying to figure out who you are, what you want to do—it's hard. It masks itself as an exciting time. And it is, of course. You finally have control over your life, to make your own decisions, to choose your path, but that doesn't mean it's easy. Most of the time, it's really, really hard." She lets go of my arm.

This time, I head to the water. Normally, I'd walk the path, take pictures of the trees, the leaves, the flowers. But today, I just sit on the grass, legs dangling over the dirt cliff that leads down to the water's edge. I close my eyes and listen to the water rushing down the river.

When I get home, I run straight upstairs to my room and open my desk drawer, then pull out the framed photo. "Here," I say to Mom, finding her in the kitchen, watering her herbs in the windowsill.

She turns. "What's this?"

"I was saving it for tomorrow, for your Mother's Day gift, but I want you to have it now. I know that this year has been all about me, and I've been so busy trying to figure out my life, I haven't really thought about how my life is affecting yours. I've been pretty much oblivious to your life, actually. I'm sorry."

"Oh honey. You're the kid, I'm the mom. I think we're doing all right." She takes the paper off the frame and looks at the photo that I captured of her and Hank in the backyard. That golden hour moment, of just the two of them together. The light glinting off their wine glasses, casting long shadows in the grass.

She studies it. "I love it. But was this—is this hard for you to see? Me and Hank?"

I shake my head. "I'm happy for you. Really."

On Sunday night, after a day hanging out with Mom and Hank and Charley, I head up to my room to work on the piece for Lisa. I read over what I wrote three times, making little tweaks here and there, then delete the whole thing. And start again.

Photographers spend a lot of time waiting. You have to to get a good shot. As a person obsessed with photography, I've spent a lot of time waiting. Waiting for the ideal light. Waiting for someone to relax. To forget I'm there. Waiting for rain to stop. Waiting for a cloud to pass. This kind of waiting—it's out of my control. It's nature, it's someone else's emotions. It's time. I have patience.

But this year I've been waiting to hear if I got into the only college I applied to. And this kind of waiting? The worst. Because I thought it was all under my control. If I just ticked all the right boxes—grades, SATs, portfolio—I'd sit back and wait to be accepted. But I got wait-listed. I got waitlisted at the only college I've ever wanted to go to. And it's also the only one I applied to. No one except my best friend knew this. She tried to tell me it was a bad idea. That I needed a backup plan. But I told her she was wrong. Turns out, she was right. I didn't get into Tisch. My whole life I've wanted to go there—at least, that's what I thought.

But the other day I was reminded that I wasn't always so obsessed with photography. It's like I had written my own history and mem-orized it. My life after my dad. I guess I did it because I missed him. Because this story I told myself was a way to bring me closer to him. It gave us a story, and one I could continue. Which is better than the alternative—a few key memories of shared moments, the details fading with time. Having this shared calling to be photographers, even if it was just a made-up story I told myself, gave me a sense of control over my past and my future. Isn't that what we all want, as our futures—this infinite unknown— lie ahead of us? We just want to feel like we have some say in what's next. Accepting that parts of my life—huge important parts—are beyond my control? It's maybe the hardest thing I've ever had to learn. But maybe the best memories, the ones that last, are the ones that happen when you stop anticipating and start participating. The photos that don't turn out, or the ones you even forget to take.

As I'm putting my bag into my locker, Dace comes up to me and wraps her arms around me. "Your piece on *Hall Pass*? I feel the exact same way. Loved it."

"Wait, it's up already?" Lisa didn't even reply to my email when I sent it to her late last night.

I pull out my phone. There it is. On the website. My byline.

I read it over, and realize Lisa didn't change a thing. Then I read the comments. There are already a bunch of comments—people all saying how brave I was to write the piece or that they were surprised to hear I got waitlisted. But the best comments are the ones where others share their own experiences about what really emerged as the theme of my piece: control.

Lisa and I bump into each other before third period. "You ran the piece."

"I told you I needed content."

"So you liked it?"

"Of course I liked it. I ran it, didn't I?"

"Well, OK. I didn't know. You didn't reply to my email or anything."

"No news is good news. When can you have the next one done?"

"The next one?"

"Yes. I need you to write as often as possible until graduation."

"Um . . ."

"Send me the next one tomorrow. Oh, and thanks, Pippa. It was just what we needed."

When I was applying to Tisch the first time around, there was a formal application, with questions and blank spaces for answers. Not that the answers were always easy, but it felt kind of like a crossword puzzle. Read the clue, write your answer in the allotted space. Not sure, skip it and come back. Writing the waitlisted essay feels like a game with no rules.

I start and delete my first sentence multiple times, and then realize I've already written what I really needed to say.

Dear Mr. Vishwanathan,

The last few weeks have been difficult, to be honest, and I can definitely say I've been doing things I wouldn't normally do. But I've also

been taking pictures. Because without photog-
raphy, I feel like a part of me is missing.

Since it's hard to sum up what I've been
doing, here's something I wrote, which I hope
explains a lot.

Then I attach my best piece from *Hall Pass*. I am
about to hit Send but then I type:

The thing is, until after our meeting, I never
realized how much time I spent only taking
photos and that I might be missing out on other
things. And while I know now that I still love
photography, I need time. Four years of college
is a big commitment, particularly to one topic,
and I want to be sure it's right for me, and I also
want to bring other experiences with me when
I do start college. I'm going to take a gap year.
Travel, see the world and photograph a lot of it.
So while I still want to go to Tisch, I'm going to
reapply next year. And see how that works out.

I add Mom and David to the BCC line and hit
Send.

Then I go downstairs. Mom and Hank are playing
Scrabble at the kitchen table and Charley's in the
basement watching a movie with José.

"Can I take the car? I'm going with Dace to get
our sleepover PJs." Somehow with everything going
on, we have left buying our PJs until the day before
the sleepover. And we *still* have no clue who we're
going to dress up as.

"Sure," Mom says, placing her tiles on the board. "Gherkins, 32 points."

I head out to the car. Ten minutes later, I knock on Dace's door. She answers, Ben right behind her. I look at the two of them and smile.

"Am I interrupting something?"

"Maybe you are," Ben says, then kisses Dace on the cheek. "Later, hot stuff." He heads out and I go inside.

"We are *so* talking about what is happening with Ben, *hot stuff*. But first: I have an idea."

"For what?" Dace says, closing the door.

"What if we get those jobs Ben's promising us at the water park for the summer. And then, in the *fall*, we travel together?"

"What do you mean, in the fall? What about Tisch?"

I shrug. "It'll be there next year."

"So let me get this straight. We'd spend the summer here, together, and then we'd spend all next year together too?"

Dace squeals and hugs me.

"So you like my anti-plan plan?"

"Well. It's not the two of us in New York. It's not me modeling and you taking pictures. We have absolutely no idea what's going to happen, but I think it's the best anti-plan plan ever. You know the main reason I loved our plan was that it meant the two of us were leaving here together. Figuring everything out together. And then when we weren't?" She sticks out her tongue and I laugh. "It was the worst." Dace swipes at a tear and then claps her hands together.

"Also, to be clear, me agreeing to stay in Spalding for the summer has *nothing* to do with the fact that I'd be seeing Ben every day."

"Obviously," I say. "Just like it has nothing to do with me seeing Dylan."

"Obviously," she says back. "All right, now that we have the next year of our lives sorted out, I have other good news to share: I have thought of our Senior Sleepover theme—Anna and Elsa. Yes, *Frozen* is pretty overdone and definitely juvenile, but think about how cozy we'll be in those flannel nighties? And the lip-sync battle? We're gonna nail it."

"I did not agree to any lip-sync battle."

"Come on. *Let it go?* It's like your actual mantra right now."

"So the Senior Sleepover," Dylan says, crossing his hands behind his head. We're in my room, Dylan lying on my bed, me on the floor, trying to fit as much stuff into my overnight bag as I can. "Is it *just* for seniors?"

"You *know* it is."

"I didn't get to go to it. Remember? I had *cancer*."

"Excuses, excuses," I say. I fold my Anna night-gown and put it in my bag, then pull my pillow out from under his head. He sits up.

"Also," he continues, "you know how you're all about the mantras? Well, I have a mantra too."

"You do not."

"I do. My mantra is Sleep." He grins. "It has been for years. I'm pretty sure we got into a lot of fights about my love of sleep, but actually, I quite enjoyed falling asleep with you at your house, that morning after the party. Which wouldn't have happened if I hadn't cleaned up your entire messy house. So Sleep."

"Actually I don't think a lot of sleep *happens* at Senior Sleepover, so you should probably just stay home in your bed if you *really* want to sleep."

"It's probably time for a new mantra anyway. What about Girlfriend. I'll just be all about my girlfriend for a while. What would you think about that?"

I grin at him. "I'm willing to let you give that one a shot."

•   •   •

Senior Sleepover is held on the football field behind the school. Tiny white lights hang the entire length of the field, from one end zone to the other. There's a makeshift stage in front of the bleachers, for the lip-sync battle. Silly games are set up here and there, like bean bag toss, and potato sack races and water balloon toss, and there's a selfie station because even a recovering Instagram snob like me loves a creative backdrop. Dace and I walk through to the other end of the field, where everyone is laying out their sleeping bags and pillows. Ours end up near Gemma and Emma and Annie, who decided to go as the girls from *Grease* after all. I unroll my sleeping bag as Dace removes a rainbow of nail polishes from her bag.

"Opening a traveling manicure business?"

"Ooooooh." She fiddles with her hair, which is

braided like Elsa's. "That is a *very* good idea. I can make money while we travel by doing manicures at the hostels. Now let me practice on you. Pink or blue?" As she paints my nails in alternating shades, I ask her about Ben.

"It's weird, right? I was so annoyed with his cocky, self-righteous attitude. But now, it's like I can see beneath that façade, how he's vulnerable and just as unsure of himself as the rest of us. You know what I mean?"

I think back to last year, when Ben first arrived at Spalding, pretending to be into photography, stealing and manipulating, and then getting to know him, and seeing how the mistakes he made came from his messed-up relationship with his father. Relatable. "Yeah, I do."

Hours later, after we've played every game, won best dressed *and* the lip-sync battle, and reminisced about four years' worth of memories, the lights are dimmed and we're all supposed to be sleeping, or at least lying in our sleeping bags and not talking, but of course that's impossible. Everyone's still up, talking and laughing in hushed tones, so there's this sort of comforting hum in the dark.

"Hey," someone says beside me and I look over to see Dylan. "Think I can squeeze in?"

"What are you doing here?" I hiss. But I could not be happier.

"You didn't really think I was going to miss out on the opportunity to snuggle into your sleeping bag, did you?" he says, squeezing himself in. My heart's pounding and he presses his face close to mine.

"How did you get in?"

"Ben Baxter could be a criminal mastermind, if he wanted to be," he says, and I look over to see Ben crawling into Dace's sleeping bag.

"So, what'd I miss?"

I wrap my arms around him. "Manicures. Bean bag toss. And—"

Before I can finish my sentence, Dylan presses his lips on mine. I close my eyes and the field gets just a bit quieter.

Nothing happens between Dylan and me in my sleeping bag, because despite what you'd think about sleeping over with your boyfriend in a football field, under the stars with only a few sleepy chaperones, I actually (eventually) fall asleep, and when I wake up, Dylan and Ben are gone.

But an hour later, we're packed up and heading out to the parking lot when Dylan pulls up. "Need a ride?"

"I have my license, thank you very much." I grin.

He grins too. "Yeah, now all you need is a car."

"I have one. Or one to use, anyway. My mom's. She stayed at Hank's so I could borrow it."

"Huh. This throws a wrench in my plans."

"Follow me home and I'll drop the car off? I forgot my toothbrush, and I want to brush my teeth before I kiss you."

"I can't argue with that."

Ten minutes later I pull into my driveway, and Dylan pulls in behind me.

"I'll just come in with you," Dylan says, following me up the driveway to the front door. "In case you need help."

"Help brushing my teeth?"

"You never know." He puts his hands around my waist.

His face is close to mine, his breath warm in my ear. I turn. "Hi."

"Hi," he says.

"Hi," a strange voice says. Dylan and I jump apart to see a guy in a blue onesie with a red tool kit. "Checking the water meter. Don't mind me."

Dylan laughs and I push open the door to the house.

"Hello?" My voice echoes in the empty house. Mom will already be at work by now.

"Cable guy's probably in the den," Dylan says, closing the door behind us and locking it.

After brushing my teeth, I find Dylan standing at the door to my room. I walk over and kiss him. And then his hands are on my face, and then they're working their way down my body. I press closer to him and lead him over to my bed. His hands explore me, and mine explore him. His skin is warm to my touch. "Do you want to . . . ?" he asks.

I nod.

Soon our bodies intertwine. We couldn't be closer together.

We must drift off to sleep because I wake up to see Dylan lying beside me.

"Hey," I say, kissing his nose.

He opens his eyes. "Hey," he says and slings his arm around me. "Good thing you brushed your teeth." His eyes shine.

"You hungry?" he asks, and I nod and we get dressed and remake my bed and then head out to the diner. I check my phone to see five texts from Dace, all the same: *Where are you???*

I reach out and grasp Dylan's hand.

Dace and Ben are still at the diner, sitting across from each other in a booth, playing cards. Dace raises her eyebrows at me. "Took a wrong turn?"

"Something like that," I say, and Dylan and I exchange a look.

She pats the seat beside her. "I saved you a seat. And ordered you your favorite. I figured you'd be hungry."

Pancakes arrive, topped with whipped cream and strawberries, and I pass Dylan a fork so we can both dig in. And maybe nothing in the history of food has ever looked and tasted better.

Dylan, Dace, Ben and I are swimming at Dace's. It's one of those perfect June days, where it's sunnier and warmer than it should be, giving a sneak peek of the summer to come. We've been lounging by the pool for hours, but I don't want the day to end. At the same time, I should leave soon, because it's Friday, and Mom and I have some *Gilmore Girls* to marathon.

I text her that I'll be home in an hour, and see an email notification—from Vishwanathan.

Dear Ms. Greene,

I was pleased to see your email and to read your essay. I think that your decision is a wise one, and I look forward to seeing your portfolio next year.

With my very best wishes,
Amir Vishwanathan

I reread the email, a smile spreading over my face, feeling good about myself, my decision and my future for the first time in a long time. Then I snap a photo of my three best friends in the pool. And jump back in.

ACKNOWLEDGMENTS

When I started writing the story of Pippa and Dylan and Dace and Ben back in 2011, I never thought it would be anything more than the one book that became *The Rule of Thirds* (ICYMI, pick it up, this book will make a lot more sense!). I am so grateful to my editor, Crissy Calhoun, who not only has the beloved double-consonant name like Ben Baxter, but more importantly loved Pippa from the start and convinced David Caron and Jack David that we needed *multiple books* to tell Pippa's story. And now, four books later, here we are. Thank you Jack, David and Crissy for this opportunity.

I have loved spending the last five years working on this series and with ECW: in particular, Jen Knoch, Susannah Ames, Troy Cunningham, Amy Smith, Jessica Albert and Tania Blokhuis. You make every little step of the process extra magical.

To my group of early readers, who offered excellent teen angst advice, especially Claudia Grieco, Gillian Grossman and Janis Leblanc.

To the coven: I'm so grateful to have found an all-girl squad of like-minded, ambitious, supportive writers: Karma Brown, Kerry Clare, Kate Hilton, Marissa Stapley, Jennifer Robson and K.A. Tucker.

To Melanie Dulos of Breakwater Publicity for reading, advice, promotion and generally being my career manager and therapist.

To my entire family for always being so interested and supportive: the Guertins (Dad and Susan, Danielle Guertin and Ron Taylor, Sarah and Rob Urbanovics, Janet Farmer) and the Shulgans (Nancy and Ron Shulgan, Jody and Mark Shulgan, Julie and Isaac Junkin).

To the Terrific Trio: Myron, Penny and Fitz for making every day more fun.

To Christopher, for reminding me every day what it feels like to be in love.

Finally, to you, the readers: I love reading every single one of your emails, comments and reviews. Your excitement is THE BEST. Thank you.

CHANTEL GUERTIN is the author of the Pippa Greene series—*The Rule of Thirds*, *Depth of Field*, *Leading Lines* and *Golden Hour*—as well as the novels *Stuck in Downward Dog* and *Love Struck*. An on-air beauty expert on *The Marilyn Denis Show*, she loves lipgloss, chocolate chip cookie dough, and anything in her favorite color: sky blue. She lives in Toronto.

Instagram & Twitter: @chantelguertin
Facebook: chantelguertinbeautybooks